Tales from

the Terrace

Robert E Harris

Forward

Peter Michaels-Saint Michael JP

England is undoubtedly the home of football
hooliganism with infamous firms all around the
country: Aston Villa (*Villa Hardcore*),
Birmingham City (*Zulu Warriors*), Derby County
(*Derby Lunatic Fringe*), Chelsea (*Chelsea
Headhunters*), Leeds United (Leeds Service
Crew), Middlesbrough (*Middlesbrough
Frontline*), Millwall (*Millwall Bushwackers*),
Newcastle United (*Gremlins*), Manchester
United *(Red Army)*, Portsmouth (*6.57 Crew*),
Tottenham Hotspur (*Yid Army*), Sheffield United
(*Blades Business Crew*), Shrewsbury Town
(English Border Front), Stoke City *(Naughty
Forty)* and West Ham United (*Inter City Firm*) to
name but a few. Even the Welsh got in on it with
Cardiff City (Soul Crew)

Described by many a plague on the national game after Liverpool FC supporters got all English teams banned from Europe. The English disease moved onto the world stage. Firms like Ajax (F -Side), Dynamo Zagreb (Bad Blue Boys), Lazio (*Irriducibili*). All following the English lead and bringing carnage to the beautiful game.

It was during this time that a firm from the lower leagues was formed by Darren Boot, Daz to his friends. A firm that follows in the traditions of hooliganism.

This book charts their rise and looks at the life of a true football hooligan, the violence, the drinking and the alcohol fuelled life style that naturally sits in this world.

The book, to some, well it is vulgar, in a none traditional way. Rather sexist (*which apparently is a thing now*) and at times crude. It comes across as degrading to the fairer sex, and even though the women were happy to be sexually used by a hooligan, is it acceptable to write it in a book? Surely the best thing to do would be to just brag about it in the golf club over drinks.

The book will make you laugh, make you think and make you see the true working of hooliganism

So, there you go, it's a book, its rude and it is funny. What more does the general public want?

Peter Michaels-Saint Michael

The Beginning

What many people don't know about me is that I was a soldier. A bloody good soldier, if I am being honest. I served in Afghanistan, Iraq, Bosnia, the Middle East and every recent war waged by HM Queen's government in modern day history. I have been awarded nine medals and a commendation for bravery.

Actually, most of that isn't true, however it proves a point, people believe what they are told. Example, you go down the Glorious Cockerel on a Friday, bang on a clean

T shirt and some young sort will believe your trash talk. She will then give you a level 1, high grade blowy, fact! And facts are like the pub bore, you can't argue with them.

Why do chicks like the hardman I hear you ask, well put simple, they like the treat em mean treat em keen sort of bloke. Makes them put the effort into a loving relationship. Chicks dig a tough man, like me, calm, cool, collected and dangerous. Even the blokes in the RAF. I know mental, I never thought it was true but believe me I have seen the ugliest, dumbest squaddie bag a tart who's what, a drunk 8 which granted is a sober 4 however he still nailed it. Walk of shame next morning giving it 'look at

me I'm Johnny Big Balls'. A how
did such a munter get so lucky?
Simple, he wears a uniform to
work, so the birds think he is
dangerous and assume he is a bad
boy.

Also, to prove I aint a
sexismist, a bird in the army I
once knew, she can get herself
some real stiff action, but
that's because blokes are suckers
for a chick that dresses up. I
know a girl from the Royal
Logistics Corps, tough old bird,
thighs like a trucker, face like
a bulldog licking piss off a
nettle. However, she is going to
be buried in a Y shaped coffin.
Loves the horizontal action and
always got them cueing up to load
her. Uniforms, danger and sex go
together like Friday night piss

up and a kebab. Made for each other.

To be brutal with you, it was one of the reasons I joined the British Army. Prior to joining I got lucky twice. Once at a party with some lass, who to be polite looked my Great Uncle Graham. After we had done the horizontal lambada I discovered she was my step sister Joanne. Still a cracking lass but looked like a poodle crossed with a Picasso. And the second time was with a girl who looked like my second cousin Samantha, sadly it turned out it was my second cousin Samantha. Cracking girl, vagina bushy like a Jackson 5 tribute act, unfortunately when we broke up it put a dampener on family gathering. What with her talking about me all the time and step sister Joanne complaining I never call her. Sort of ruined my Nans funeral party weekend in Skegness. Bless her only 46, no age to be hit by a bus. Ironically a number 46 bus. Cracking send of though, despite the sly looks I got from the laides.

When we were all together, I looked like Cinderella, with the two ugly sisters either side of me. But ask any man, a result counts regards of the state of the bird, even if you later discover you are distantly related.

So anyway, I was an ordinary sort of lad, you know the type. Tall,

not overly pretty, no real formal
qualifications to mention. A
distinct lack of ambition or
talent in equal measures. So, I
think to myself one day. Which
isn't too strange because you
can't think to another person.
So, I think to myself, why not
join the army, get a job, travel
a bit and move out my step dads
one bedroomed compact flat. Get
away from the family, become a
real man.

I thought about it and after the
recruiter down at the Army
careers told me all I could do
was join the infantry, I decided
to join the infantry.

Was it a good idea? I get to
sleep in fields, drink loads with

the lads and get muddy? Ideal for a working-class kid that once lived in a field for a week, due to crowded housing market and being smashed off my nut on cheap supermarket lager, after me mate Diaz had a fifteenth birthday party down at the local youth club.

I rocked up to the Depot and got shouted at for weeks on end by right big buggers. Did loads of running and PE and finally got me hands on some weapons. Was cracking time, also in the army you have three meals a day, never heard of anyone having three meals a day before, thought I was Prince of Wales or something.

So, a month or so in I gets to go on leave, and I go to my home town, couldn't think of where else to go. I was right excited. Granted not many people are happy to go to Brompton, but, its where I grew up and me family lived there.

I got off the train and walked to me Mom's house. Once there our Debbie said come to the pub, so I got changed and went down to the Shining Pond. We were chatting about stuff and my work and that, one of the more mature barmaids, Gayle, well she gazed at me with her good eye, and looked at the door with the other eye. I knew she was feeling fruity by the way she was polishing that pint glass, as she held in her overly wart ridden hand.

Later I went to the toilet and as I came out of the cubicle, Gayle limped in, her arthritic leg dragging only slightly behind her. I casually said to her "I'd give it five minutes love." Pointing to the cubicle, as the odour started to circulate and make the air heavy and somewhat acidic. To which she retched a little, she looked at me with her good eye and said to me in her broad Yorkshire accent "have you shat a dead skunk, you dirty git." Our eyes locked, well the good one locked her other eye was looking in the mirror. Gayle lunged at me like a starving gazelle and she pushed me back into the cubicle, after I gave it a second flush, bit of a floater hanging around, Gayle kneeled down and gave me a real blowy.

Full on, straight on it she was. Her missing front teeth helping me glide into her nicotine-stained mouth with ease. That girl could suck start a Harley Davidson. Well within minutes I gave her a shot of my muck, she swallowed my love offering like a piss head doing shots and then she looked at me with a hint of jaundice and sexual satisfaction. She licked her lips, got off of her knees and limped out of the toilet, straight back behind the bar, pulling pints. She probably should have washed her hands, but I'm no Health and Safety snitch.

It was at that moment I realised:

A: Ken was in the next cubicle
taking a dump.

B: Having great stories and being
a hard man gets the girls moist.

I was so happy and overjoyed I
washed my hands before going back
to the bar, I was proper buzzing,
I bought myself a vodka with
lager chaser I also got our
Debbie a drink, a bottle of
Castaway, believe me they weren't
cheap.

My life was changed forever. Or
so I thought.

I was discharged from the Army on week 9 of training due to differences of opinion, I thought I was physically fit and the Army thought I was asthmatic. So, my life was in ruins, or was it?

Estate

After I left the army, I went
back to my home town in Yorkshire
and got myself a lovely, and more
to the point, cheap council flat
on the Parkinson Estate.

It is an ordinary sort of inner-
city council estate, massively
over crowded, low-to no income
families, single parents as far
as the eyes could see and dogs
barking all hours of the day and
night. A burnt-out mark 2 Ford
Fiesta was used as a climbing
frame by the young kids during
the day, and a hangout for
teenagers at night to smoke roll
ups and drink cheap cider.

I lived at flat number 56, a lovely two bedroomed compact flat, with a balcony, like the one the Queen has at Buckingham Palace, I assume the Queens balcony had less bird shit on hers, but there you go. The flat had all the modern fittings, you know, a Sky Dish, indoor toilet. A security system on the main door to stop unwanted people coming into the block, unless they lived there obviously. It was a cracking place and only a two-minute walk to the Glorious Cockerel public house, result.

The Glorious Cockerel pub was a typical urban estate bar. Serving all day breakfast 12 until 3 every day, except Sundays. It did a decent pint; the landlord was a young woman called Naomi. She was

a normal forty Benson and Hedges
a day, slutty dressed, foul
mouthed, jewellery wearing
landlord. Salt of the earth when
sober, the type that would do
anything for you, except lend you
money.

Naomi has a boyfriend Col,
cracking fella. She previously
had a husband but they separated
some years ago. They separated
due to differences of opinions,
and her catching him back
scuttling a barmaid over the pool
table after hours. It put a real
dampener on the whole marriage.
She filed for divorce and he, on
his release from hospital, he
moved to his mothers in
Scunthorpe. The barmaid still
works there, but that's sisters
for you, they stick together.

Her fella Col, he was a tallish well to do man, only one criminal conviction to his name, a solid reliable chap. He loved Naomi with all his heart, partly because she was a beautiful woman with a firm body, and she was apparently a good ride, and partly out of fear; but together they worked. He was a calm and relaxed man who wore a mullet with pride. She was a gob shite Paddy with a right nice shitter and she was definitely in charge of that relationship.

The décor of the bar was very mid-eighties chic. It had a picture of Her Majesty the Queen behind the bar. A Union Jack on the main wall near the pool table. An Irish Tricolour on the back wall. There were a couple of pictures of horses, scattered around the walls and loads of pictures of Dublin, Naomi was a proud Paddy. Behind the bar there was a picture of some topless woman, it was there to try and sell men peanuts, the more peanuts you bought the more of her body was revealed, Old Dirty Barry spent so much on peanuts try to get to see the birds' baps, but he had to stop when he developed a peanut allergy, it broke his little heart.

The carpet in the bar was a shade of brown only ever seen in pub carpets. Starfish Mocha I believe is the official correct colour.

On a Thursday and a Friday there was a disco run by Disco Danny, lovely man, fat thing though, looked like a capital D. He had the biggest selection of Hawaiian shirts anywhere in the North of England. Lovey bloke, he'd do anything for you, as long as it didn't involve any effort on his behalf. He had all the banter and was popular with the ladies. Well, he was popular amongst the over fifties, but despite their looks and facial hair they were still technically women.

On Saturday the bar had Karaoke, Danny's younger brother Keith ran that. He was like Danny to a point, except two feet smaller and slightly fatter, and not so good with the banter. He didn't need it though; he was married to Scabies Sharon; she was a lovely girl despite the excessive eczema

and tendency to fight anything
after six pints.

On Sundays it was Sunday Funday,
which meant, a disco with
karaoke. In summer they had a
bouncy castle outside in the car
park, to keep the kids
entertained and that. Cracking
night Sunday.

Monday was Quiz night, and
buffet, all the lads got together
threw some arrows and had a bit
of banter, then tried to win
eight pints on the quiz. Not as
easy as it sounds, what with most
of the lads educationally
deprived.

Tuesday was Pool League at home every other week, opposite week was an away fixture, they were always good nights and a good laugh, win or lose. To be fair mainly lose as we only tuned up for the lager and free sandwiches.

Wednesday was lady's night, which usually meant the girls would get all dressed up, go down the bar and talk about men, and shopping, you know usually girly stuff. It usually ended with Candice crying down her phone to her Terry, telling him someone had said something to her, there would be an argument and usually the police would get called. Terry would turn up, give it the big I am, then get a punch off Naomi.

Like I say, cracking normal run
of the mill pub.

The estate, well the landing to
the left of the one I lived was
called 'no man's land', simply
because none of the women that
lived there were married. My
landing housed ten families, and
the landing to my right was home
to twenty-two families. All salt
of the earth people. Proper
people, you know the type, not
once was there a burglary on our
estate. Our thieves had respect;
they would go to another area to
rob. Now that is genuine respect,
something that is missing from
society these days.

Two doors down from me was Mental
Nicky, lovely fella, he was

married to Shaniqua, the local
hairdresser at Slick and Twisted,
local gossip and know it all.
They had two kids Carl and Clint.
Nicky was old school proper skin
head. Tattoos everywhere, he even
had his own name tattooed inside
his lip. He only ever wore knock
off Fred Perry T-shirt. His arm
tattoos consisted mainly of the
names of ex-girlfriends, many of
whom still lived on the estate.
Hard as nails he was, and
borderline psychotic, but he
loved his missus and kids so not
all bad. His proudest day was
getting mistaken for a football
fan by some hooligans from
Chelsea, they kicked the shit out
of him. Nicky always maintains it
was the best day of his life, out
ranking his wedding day and the
birth of his two children.

Whenever he told the story he got all animated and turned on.

Shaniqua was a natural blonde, with dark black roots. Her tattoos were a lot classier than Nicky's; she had a swallow on one arm and the letter I above it? On the other arm a pair of scissors with a Latin phrase underneath praeciderat supra, turns out it means a 'cut above' that woman was pure class.

She had a body that many forty-year-old women would be proud of, shapely legs, firm-ish tits, and not too much of a muffin top. The sort of woman that still looked good in a tight black dress down at the Saturday night disco, from

a distance. Classy in a slutty
sort of way, you know the type.

On the other side of me lived
Sandra, she was a lovely old
dear, seventy-three years young.
She still smoked sixty cigs a
day, drank stout and loved a good
old natter. She would pop round
to mine some days, with a plate
of food, bless her. We'd sit
there having a laugh chatting
away before it was time to go to
the pub. He favourites topics of
conversation were the good old
days. Her viewpoints are today
considered racist and homophobic,
but in her day those sorts of
views were more acceptable, and
she was too old to change.

Burglar Barry lived a few doors down, lovely man. He could get his hands on anything, no questions asked. It was Barry that got me my sofa, fridge, sky box, microwave, bed and carpets, £200 job lot, see what I mean real people.

There were many single parents on the estate, mainly due to buy one get one free down the Blue Lion on the high street. The pub was actually called the White Lion, but on a Wednesday £15 entry, free lager, spirit and mixer or cider all night long, and after a few cheeky ones the ladies went a bit sexually mental, they'd part with their knickers quicker than you could say 'alright love'. Many a child was conceived in the

Blue Lion's disabled toilets on a
Wednesday night.

The estate had a above national
average of children with ADHD,
but only because Disability
Living Allowance paid up for that
sort of thing. As soon as a child
could walk the mother would bang
a claim in. Day of the
assessment, youngster was given a
can of red bull and a bar of
chocolate. Result. Every time
they got the money. It made more
sense though, rather than give
the money away to scroungers.

I loved the estate; it had a
high-quality feel to it. It had
more England Flags than Wembley
stadium and more skin heads than
a man could count. There was

always something going on, you
had everything from, a street
party to police attending a
weekend domestic. Old Sarah
bellowing "I love you babes" to
Luke as she was being placed into
a police car. Every other
weekend she spent in the cells,
then on Monday she'd come out,
give Luke some kinky sex. He'd
drop the charges and their love
would continue,

I did always wonder why the
police took Sarah away, as it was
always Luke dropping the charges
on a Monday, but she got fed in
the cells so she wasn't that
bothered, and Luke had to look
after the triplets. Bless Luke,
he was rather skinny and weak,
all ten stone of him, where as
she was built like a brick shit

house, she had to be a minimum of
twenty stone, when sober, hey but
they truly loved and respected
each other, like a modern-day
Romeo and Juliet love story.

Getting Started

So, there I was one day, sat in the Glorious Cockerel, having a few drinks, minding my own. In walked Mental Nicky, he got himself a pint and sat down uninvited at my table.

It was a nothing sort of day, Horse Racing was on the big screen, Micky the Tip was advising everyone what to bet on. He had a win ratio of one win a week, but people still took his advice. In his defence he knew how to play the fruit machine, you bang a few quid in, Micky appears gets you to hold your plums and you're on a winning streak.

Mental and me got chatting about life, how it was hard to find a job, especially if you had a criminal record like Nicky and no qualifications, like Nicky.

Nicky always maintained it was because of foreigners that he couldn't get a job, not his convictions for violence, theft, fraud, criminal damage or the fact he couldn't speak a sentence without saying 'fuck' at least three times. Council Tourette's affected most people where I lived.

Anyway, we got talking about football, and we got on to the time Chelsea fans kicked lumps out of Nicky. He got a real buzz out of it, he had a semi on

telling me the story, which was
rather disturbing and put me
right off my pork scratchings.

So, after a bit of banter I said
to him, we should get our own
firm up and running, it will give
us something to do on a Saturday
afternoon, and the birds well,
come on they'd be begging for it.
Chicks bless em, they say they
want a gentleman, but reality is
they want a bastard that will
kick the shit out of a chav for
them. They want a man to be a
man, someone who will bang her
tidy on a Friday night, but look
after her kids Saturday morning
whilst she does a big shop. You
know proper man.

Our local football team was a shower of shit called AFC Brompton, however just across from the ground there was a pub so we decided to start a firm and follow AFC Brompton.

We sat there for hours talking through our manifesto, which was: get pissed, shag birds and fight, very similar to a Friday night if I am being honest with you. The most important thing about a firm is the name we spent hours trying to think of a decent name as it is that important. West Ham United - Inter City Firm (ICF), Chelsea - Head-hunters, Leicester City - Baby Squad, Tottenham Hotspur - Yid Army, Sheffield United Blades Business Crew (BBC). A name has to stand out and sound impressive.

We went through a series of
names, to be fair they all
sounded shit. After a few hours
and several pints, we got it down
to two. Brompton Hard Squad or
Brompton Life Takers

We settled for Brompton Life
Takers or BLT for short. We
decided on life takers, one
because we could fight and two,
just because Nicky always used to
say he was a heart breaker and
life taker, not sure why he ever
said that. Also, Brompton Hard
Squad would have been BHS, and
that sounded stupid.

Later that day I spoke with
Burglar Barry and arranged for
him to drop off some knock off
Stone Island gear. If you're

going to be a hooligan you need the uniform. Unfortunately, Barry was a little drunk when I told him and he thought I said something about a Stone in Ireland, so he dropped off ten 'I Kissed the Blaney Stone' Sweatshirts, the twat. Still got them, impossible to sell in Yorkshire. He eventually sobered up and got me the right items, dozy sod.

Anyway, we got them eventually, so the following night I wore my Stone Islands top and went to the Blue Lion for a few two for ones before heading to the Cock for the disco.

As soon as the door opened, I walked in with that Swagger only seen on people who think they are Liam Gallagher. We call them, twats, people that swagger when they walk like the Mancunian Candidate, not sure why though?

Everyone was looking at me, top boy was in the house. I walked up to the bar, looked the old dear in the eyes, and ordered a pint. She leaned over the bar and gave me a real hard slap around my head, "say please you mouthy twat." She proper rattled at me. I was a little stunned, so I tried again this time I said please, old Zoe was a rough old tart and she could slap like a heavy weight boxer, hands like sandpaper. I was only glad she was my mom, otherwise she'd have properly laid me out for being rude.

I had a good few beers in the
Blue Lion, chatted to a mate of
mine Nosher. Have to admit Nosher
is a lovely girl old and slightly
haggard but the sort of bird,
that after a few you'd have a go
on. Even though she is a little
bit crude at times.

Nosher got her nickname after
being banned from the all you can
eat Chinese restaurant Chow Mein
Mao's. She once ate enough food
for six men, then threw up on the
spring rolls. All this before
giving a blow job to one of the
waiting staff in the girls'
toilets.

I have known Nosher for many
years, she is the school crossing
lady at the local primary school,
you can see her every morning
swearing at the drivers if they
don't slow down, she gets really
lippy if she is hungover. She
genuinely loves and cares for
those kids, despite some of the
names she calls them. She didn't
have kids herself due to her
husband having a sperm count so
low, that when he came dust shot
out of him. Shame really because
Nosher was one of those naturally
caring birds.

From there I headed to the Cock,
for the disco. On arrival
Mongoose Mick collared me. Word
had got out about Brompton Life
Takers and he wanted in. I
naturally said yes, more the

merrier. However, Nicky said he had to do an initiation test to be accepted. The test was he had to rest his head on the pool table and have a white ball shot at it. It sounded like a good laugh so I told him that's what he had to do. Nicky lined up the cue ball, chalked his stick as Micky rested his head on the greenish beer-stained table. Nicky took aim and fired that ball as hard as he could and after three attempts finally the white balls smashed into his head. This caused Mongoose to cry out in pain and me and Nicky cry with laughter. He passed the test and BLT was finally up and running.

Mongoose was a decent lad, long term unemployed due to

illiteracy, a criminal record, oh and the ubiquitous bad back. He 'injured' his back once doing community service at an older people's home. He took a few quid in compensation and has been a slave to his injury ever since. Well, I say ever since it flairs up once a year around the time he has to redo his Disability Living Allowance claim. His adopted parents called him mongoose, something to do with when he was a kid. He was the only person I ever met that actually looked adopted.

We spent the night having some cheeky lagers, and looking at the fixtures for Brompton AFC. Most of the games look like they would be shite, but the local derby game against Wakefield looked

like it good be a good day out.
Most games were local-ish and one
or two down south, playing the
mockneys. The sort of bloke that
lives near London so adopts that
apples and pears shite.

For those people that don't know
Wakefield, it has a great night
life, many decent bars and some
right slappers go out there, it's
on par with Essex for growlers.
It would be like shooting snatch
in a basket. Even someone as
sexually handicapped as Mongoose
would be able to get a bunk up.

That night some of the ladies in
the Glorious Cockerel were
hovering around us. Word was
starting to spread that we had
started a firm and you know how

it is, a lady loves a hard man.
How do you think Ross Kemp got
laid so much?

I ended up leaving the Cockerel
with Debbie, a delightful young
minx. She once went on a school
trip to London and when she came
back, she was so cosmopolitan and
travelled. She spoke with her own
version of cockney slang, that
took ages to say what she
actually meant, I wouldn't mind
but she was only in London for
four hours. We just chatted as I
walked her home. She told me I
was a right dogs wag, turns out
that was her way of saying shag?
Mad old tart but a right tight
arse on her. So, swings and
roundabouts.

She hadn't in all the years let
herself go, to be fair there
wasn't much to let go of. She had
teeth like council bins, one
brown, one green and one missing,
decent body for a bird who had
churned out five kids. Granted
she had Lip injections to plump
up her mouth after the benefits
agency backdated one of the kids
claims for the ADHD. But the
trout pout sort of suited her,
despite the slight green puss
leaking out the side.

We spoke about how her Tony left
her when she was pregnant with
Kai. And how her previous fella
Walt left her when the child Karl
was born, Karl appeared to be of
a different ethnic background to
Walt, to this day Walt maintains

he has never even been to Korea,
never mind had Korean relatives.

Debbie had been let down by all
the fathers of her five children.
Frank Welds, the local smack rat,
let her down on three separate
occasions, when Kylie was born,
Kandy and the last one Kelly, but
Debbie took him back each time
because 'He did have a good sense
of humour.' However, each time
Franks wife got wind of the
relationship and it kicked off.
Frank always went running back to
his wife, but that's true love
for you. Say what you want about
Frank, he is a romantic old fool.

When we got back to Debbie's
flat, I gave her a peck on the
cheek, and walked slowly to my

flat, day dreaming of being a football hooligan, whilst Debbie screamed down the landing that I was a gay. All because I didn't try it on with her, that's a proper feminist for you.

The only reason I didn't try it on with her was I saw her earlier that day at *Buy the Way*, the local corner shop, buying some tampons. No point trying to blag some snatch when there is a crimson tide in tuna bay. Found out the next day the Tampons weren't for Debbie they were for old Denise her mate, she got caught short with the red mess, couldn't nip to shop for herself especially as she had white jeans on when she got the call. I was felt red faced I can tell you.

The next day Mongoose called round, I had promised to sell him a Stone Island sweatshirt. I paid £50 for ten, so I sold Mongoose one for forty pounds. I like Mongoose, but my unemployment benefit had run out and I needed cash for the Friday night disco. I also forgot to tell Mongoose they were knock off, he still to this day thinks his forty-pound Stone Islands top is genuine.

Barry would always claim they were genuine, I was convinced they weren't genuine, because Stone Island don't sell their gear in Sainsburys bags. Stone Island also never called their brand Stone Islands. But they were cheap so no harm no foul.

Friday day was a drag, I had nothing to do and it was raining outside, so I stayed in a masturbated to Loose Women, it was a tough one but somehow I managed it. However, in the evening, I had a shower, put on some of my knock off Hugo Boss aftershave, my God the stuff doesn't half burn when you whack it on, I wore a clean Stone Islands top and a pair of skinny jeans and a pair of Adidas Gazelle trainers. I must admit I looked amazing, once I added my gold platted necklace, I was a dead ringer for a young George Clooney.

The Cock was heaving, everyone loved Friday night on the estate, and most people had got their Unemployment. Which meant it was

going to be a mental night. The
disco was banging, Best of Kylie
was being played, her early stuff
not the shit she sings now.

Some of the girls were on the
dance floor dressed like models
from down south. When the ladies
on the estate got dressed up,
they actually wore less clothes
than normal, which was a result.
Every woman on the dance floor
had a skirt so short their arse
was hanging out. To be fair some
of them could wear ankle length
skirts and their arse would still
be hanging out. But they looked
classy.

Mental Nicky was at the bar
giving some young lad the evil
stare, it turns out the young lad

had walked past Nicky and glanced up at Shaniqua. She was wearing a low-cut top and her ample baps were on show. Nicky took offence to the lad having a look at them and so we had to sort him.

After a few minutes the lad went to the toilets so me, Mental and Mongoose followed him in. Mental pulled him for looking at Shaniqua. The lad in question didn't have a clue, he told Mental he just glanced up because it was busy at the bar and he didn't want to walk into anyone. Mental went well erm, mental; he went full scale all out crazy on him. Grabbed this lad round the neck and starts screaming at him for ignoring his missus and thinking her tits were shite. He was fuming the lad didn't find

her baps attractive. Enough was
enough and his lack of respect
for Shaniqua meant he had to take
a kicking.

The lad shit himself Mental
punched him a few times and he
eventually went down, when he
slumped to the floor, I kicked
him twice in the back. The kicks
were quite hard, I hurt my toes a
little. As he laid there, Mental
pulled out a card and laid it on
him, before we walked out.

Turns out Mental had a mate Nat
who was a printer, so he had some
calling cards made out for the
firm. Pure class, they read '*you
have just had a taste of the
BLT*'. Priceless.

We walked out of the toilets proud as punch after the firms first official run out. The lad we smacked walked out the toilets a few seconds after we did, he gave us the two fingers and ran out the pub, cheeky twat.

Word got round the pub that we had run a kid out, mainly as Mental told everyone in great detail what we had done. The night was proper crazy, everyone was in a top mood. Well except Shaniqua she'd been down to the beauty parlour *Change the Ring Tone*, and had anal bleaching, apparently her hoop was twitching like mad so she spent most of the evening in the ladies, splashing cold water on her hoop.

This one girl Gaynor bought me a
pint and was dead flirty with me.
We took to the dance floor and
did the Macarena together before
leaving for her place. It was
obvious I was getting some off
her when we got back. Doing the
Macarena around our way with
someone of the opposite sex is
like announcing you're exclusive.
It's one step away from getting
matching tattoos.

Unfortunately, though on the way
back we walked past the Horse and
Groom pub and who was outside but
the lad from the pub earlier.
Only this time he was there with
two other student mates. Once he
had clocked me, they ran up to me
to beat the crap out of me, I
somehow managed to do a runner, I
got about two yards up the road

when I tripped over a traffic
cone and grazed my knee. Before
taking a proper kicking by the
three lads. Gaynor the slag,
ended up going back to one of the
student's house for a party and
as it turns out, to get fingered.

I suppose as a top boy, you give
out a beating and sometimes you
have to take a beating, it's all
part of the game. All in all,
though it was a good night and a
buzz having a tear up was
amazing.

Next morning, I woke up with a
banging hangover and one of my
neighbours Frank was making some
right noise. I couldn't complain
though, he is a World War Two
veteran. Fought for his country,

therefore you had to respect the old git.

I had to be up early that day it was the Brompton Life Takers first game, at home to Spalding FC. I was so excited and nervous I had to crack one off in the shower. Turns out I was that excited, it only took a couple of flicks to finish me off.

I popped round to Franks for a brew and some banter to pass the time. I really liked Frank, would spend hours telling me of his time in the army and his travels through Europe. The hardship and the battles he took part in. How he served his country with pride.

He served his time in the 24th Panzer Division, he got captured by the British in Africa. When I say captured, he gave himself up as he didn't like fighting, after his leg was shot up. Frank eventually fell in love with a NAAFI maid and stayed in the UK after the war. His wife Doris von Vormann (nee Mullins) was a lovely woman and she made a cracking full English.

Frank and Doris had two daughters Eva and Edda, beautiful sorts, Eva was a bit of a bitch, but she had an arse so tight you could bounce her off the wall, so you ignored the mood swings, evil stares and bitchy comments. She was a business woman, she ran *Nice Baps*, a sandwich shop down on the parade, and she had *Shaven*

Haven which was a boutique and
waxing salon. Edda the younger
sister was a very shy character,
and by all accounts, overcome
with frigidity, shame really as
she was a looker. She was skinny,
blonde haired, blue eyed but her
shyness and frigidity put many
fellas off. She never actually
had a boyfriend, whereas Eva, she
was a very popular with married
men, or men who had a few quid,
but as I said she was a business
woman.

First Game

I was both edgy and excited for our first game, I got dressed and headed down to the Cock for a livener. I had on a knock off Burberry baseball cap, a knock off Stone Islands sweatshirt, some stretch jeans and a beautiful pair of knock off Adidas Samba. I must admit I looked the part, I looked like a million dollars, and my entire outfit cost less than forty quid, thanks to burglar Bill.

Down at the Cock, Mental and Mongoose were already at the bar, they were kitted out in knock off gear. Mongoose brought his cousin Shaba Frank with him. He got his nickname a few years earlier.

Every week down at the Cock Friday night Disco whenever Mr Loverman came on old Frank would get up and give it large on the dancefloor. A great nickname, a bit of a dig but it suited him. He was a lovely bloke, wrong side of sixty but keen for a fight and loved a party so he was in.

We had a few pints and headed to the ground; Brompton's home ground was the Palin Stadium, down on Clarkson Street. It was a little run down and shit to be fair. Only one stand had a roof on it, that was the *Abra Kebabra* Stand. It was the posh people went, me and the boys were heading for the Kop, for proper fans. First, we called into the pub opposite the ground.

The Starfish and Truffle was a nice pub, sort of place you'd take a lady if you were wanting to get serious with her. Or you fancied a nice meal to moisten her upper leg regions. All the food was reasonably priced, Scampi and Chips £4.00, Cheese Burger and Chips £4.00, Turkey Twizzlers and beans £2.50, proper nice gastro pub. Classy place, all the walls were painted an off shade of Snatch Pink, with an ivory trim. It was very welcoming. The pictures on the wall were all from yester year, old fellas pushing carts and that. It felt a proper quality place.

Inside there was only about twenty people in, including the five staff and a Staffordshire

Bull Terrier called Bruno. Mental
asked the landlord when the
football crowd would be in, to
which she replied 'you're already
here, dickhead'. Not a great
start but they did a decent drop
of stout at the Starfish so not a
complete waste of time.

Just after three pm we headed to
the ground. No self-respecting
hooligan gets there before three.
We walked in and took our place
at the back of the Kop, not a
great choice, because every time
the ball went out of play the
keeper would shout us to get it.
We'd have to run to the front of
the Kop throw him the ball then
head back up. Saying that it kept
me fit. On the away end Spalding
had brought a right firm. There
was BLT with four hooligans and

Spalding's firm must have been
fifteen sixteen strong and a
Cocker Spaniel.

We spent the entire game chanting
abuse to them and their players;
it was all good harmless fun and
banter. Then the magic started.
Bang on full time, we ran down to
the front and legged it across
the pitch. Well, the others did I
was worn out from fetching the
ball every five minutes, I got to
the half way line and I was
breathing out my arse, so I
stopped to get my breath. Mental
wasted no time and went wading in
smacking this lad from Spalding
straight in the chest. Mongoose
was kicking the day lights out of
this young lad, and Shaba was
getting kicked senseless by two
blokes and an old woman. By the

time I walked over, I managed to
kick one of their fans on the
leg. Then two security guards and
a police officer came over so we
legged it out the ground and down
the road to safety. All four of
us were on a high from the rush
of it all. That was it I was
hooked on the lifestyle. Oh, and
Brompton lost six nil to
Spalding.

That night we went to the
Cockerel for the disco. We were
proper heroes, all the boys
wanted to be us and some of the
rougher women wanted to sleep
with us. Shaba Frank pulled a
right little darling, old Ethel
Ringwald only 67 years young, but
had the body and face of a woman
much older. After a couple of
pints, he did the Turkey trot

with Ethel, you know, once round
the dance floor then outside for
a gobble.

I got talking to No Morals Sally.
She was a twenty something,
decent sort, only two kids so not
a full-on slag, however she would
do anything, I mean anything
after a few shandies. Both her
kids lived with their fathers
from Thursday until Monday, so
Sally could have a rest and get
pissed with the girls. Liam the
father of the oldest was in the
pub with his new girl Gail and
Sally's oldest child Monique.
There were no hard feelings
between Gail and Sally, well how
could there be they were cousins,
and family is family.

Sally was well impressed with my stories of battle, she kept running her body up against me. I was not sure if she was turned on or doing the Lambada, sometimes it is hard to tell.

We had a few cheeky drinks and finished the night off dancing to Agadoo on the dance floor. Before I escorted her home.

When got back to her flat, she gave me a passionate kiss on the lips, before pushing me to one side and vomiting all over my new Adidas Sambas. She then continued to passionately kiss me for a few more minutes, then she stopped, wiped her mouth clean and walked in her flat, giving me a cheeky wink before slamming the door

shut. I went home alone, with a
semi. Leaving a trail of her
vomit behind me and my trainers
stinking of wine and Sambuca. I
tell you with that stench it was
a tough wank when I got back,
however always the professional,
I managed it.

The following week was very
uneventful, I spent most of it
trying to wash the vomit and
odour out of my trainers. I
manged to get some more knock off
gear from Barry. I also got a
mobile phone off him to, £30 job
lot.

That weekend was our first away
game. Brompton were going to
Pontefract City in the early
stages of the FA Cup. So, I had

to save some cash for the big day. Mental Nicky called round a few days before to go over the plans. He also informed me we had two new members to our firm.

Big Jock Wilson, he wasn't Scottish he once wore a jockstrap to school as a kid and everyone took the piss, ever since then he has been called Jock. The title Big came about when his ex-girlfriend Brenda shared a dick pic, he sent her. You had to really zoom in to see is pride n joy. People said the term Big was ironic, not knowing what that means I just say it's a piss take.

Mandy Peters was the other member, now personally I have

read many books on hooligans and none mention women. I told Nicky this but he pointed out that she wanted to join and no one had the nerve to tell her no. She had previously served time for biting a man's penis. In her defence she did tell him not to come in her mouth. Her only defence in court was 'no one shoots their muck in my mouth until were engaged.' She got six months.

Mandy was a big girl, both in height and width, and she had a tattoo on the forearm of a pint of cider. Lovely girl though, cracking sense of humour and loyal as a Labrador puppy. She also had the brains of a Labrador puppy, but no one ever described Mandy as cute.

That Saturday, I got dressed, Stone Island Sweatshirt, skinny jeans and clean Samba trainers. Mobile phone in my pocket and a splash of Boss ooh the toilet, obviously it was knock off, when first applied, my god it burned, people outside my flat must have thought I was yodelling. Once the stinging and redness wore off I went down the Cockerel to meet the firm.

We looked like a proper firm Nicky in his knock off Fred Perry t shirt, Mongoose in a Tommy Hills Fingers knock off sweatshirt, Shaba had on a raincoat? And Mandy was wearing some jumper from Primark that was obviously a size to small. Big Jock was a no show, his wife Eileen got proper moody on.

Night before Jock got a bit worse for wear and took the Dexy's song Come On Eillen a little too literal. Two AM and Eileen is rudely awakened by Jock glazing her like a Danish.

The lads ragged me a bit at the bar, due to the smell of the Boss knock off aftershave, and the fact I had lemonade in my lager. I read in a book all top hooligans drink Lager Top so that's what I ordered, basically it is lager with a splash of lemonade in it. It's a hard bastards Lager Shandy. I tried it, it was the dogs. The gang started taking the piss calling me some very derogative names, some of which were in the current political climate rather homophobic. But it was just

banter amongst friends, they all
know I have never packed fudge in
my entire life.

We finished our drinks and got
the bus to Pontefract. Took
bloody ages to get there. The bus
was horrible it stank of piss, I
later discovered Mandy squatted
at the back of the bus and had a
piss. It took ages to get the
smell of asparagus out me nose.

When we finally arrived, we went
into town and had a few drinks.
We used the time to scope out the
opposition. To be fair there
wasn't that much. It was market
day and the pub was full of old
dears. We stood out like soar
thumbs; the local ladies could
smell new DNA and they were

giving us the eye. We got
chatting to one old dear, and she
kindly walked us to the ground.
It had a similar look to the
Coliseum in Rome. It wasn't
majestic or imposing. It was a
big fucking ruin. What a dump.

Inside the ground we were joined
on the away end by a local police
officer, we thought our
reputation has arrived before us.
Turns out he had to be there,
because there was more than three
of us. Nice bloke though, that
copper was.

The Bovril was a touch expensive
and the meat pie didn't contain
much meat. Except for that it was
an ok afternoon. The standard of
football was rubbish, but we won.

One nil, a Pontefract own goal.
Was funny really the ball was
cleared off the line by their
keeper, but it hit the defender
on the back of the head an went
in. Shaba went running down to
the front to take the piss out of
the keeper, but he tripped half
way down and bounced down the
terrace. Mandy laughed so much
she dropped her meat pie, which
put her in a right mood. The
police officer laughed at Mandy's
misfortune, so Mandy being Mandy
punched him.

Within a minute half a dozen
police turn up and Mandy is
arrested. It took most of the
second half for the police to
remove her from the ground, for a
fat lass, she was pretty fit and
put up a right fight. She was

later charged with four counts of
assault on police and Section
Four public Order Act. She ended
up getting three years
imprisonment for it. On the day
she got sent down we all promised
to visit her, although to be fair
none of us ever did.

After the game we left the
ground, went to the bus station
and waited for the bus to take us
home. Whist waiting, some local
biker gang rode past on their
bikes giving us the evils and
sticking two fingers up. So, we
ran at them, don't know why we
did because those BMXs can move
at speed, we had no chance
catching them. And the kids on
them were much younger and fitter
than us. So, I kicked a bin over

instead, there was litter
everywhere. Was proper good fun.

We got back to the Cockerel and
told everyone about our day out
and how I trashed the city
centre, kicking that bin over,
old Debbie was well impressed.
She came over to me and whispered
in my ear "I'm not ragged up."
Boom, no period meant the gates
to the promised land were
officially open. I know there and
then I was on for a bunk up. We
stayed chatting and flirting
until last orders, then nipped
down to *In Cod I Trust*, for a bag
of chips. Then it was off to
Debbie's for a proper fish
supper.

Debbie's flat was mint, she had Sky Tv, massive flat screen Television and her sofa had original covers on. We sat on the sofa for a bit and I gave her a quick finger blast to lubricate her before we went to the bedroom.

Inside her bedroom, I pushed her dirty washing off the bed, got undressed and jumped in. Debbie had been to the bathroom to freshen up. She came in the room, slipped out of her jumpsuit to reveal a cracking set of baps. Granted when she took off the wonder bra, they sagged quite a bit, but hey, having loads of kids suck the life out of them will do it to most tits.

I got myself a condom and put it on, Debbie was taken aback at first, started shouting at me that I thought she was a skank with STD's and that. I calmed her down and informed her that my spunk was well powerful and I didn't think knocking her up first night was a good idea. She calmed down and gave me some manual help getting my love wand up to performance level. I ventured south and gave her some tongue action. To be fair it reminded me of the time I dropped my kebab outside *Abra Kebabra*.

Whilst plating her I could taste the lemon wet wipe she had used to spruce herself up. Lemon and damp vagina had a rather unique pungent smell, a bit like the Boss aftershave I wore earlier, but I sort of liked it. I then climbed on top of her, and entered her overgrown garden of love.

  Within minutes I had serviced her and emptied my load. I quickly got up, flicked my condom onto the floor next to her dirty underwear and got dressed. Debbie had crashed out, to be fair I think she was already asleep before I had cum. I left her flat and went home a very happy chap. I assumed Debbie was sexually satisfied and I know I definitely was. Great day out, great night, and I got some. Was great being a fully-fledged hooligan.

The next morning Debbie came round shooting her mouth off,

apparently her youngest had
slipped on my used condom and
hurt his ankle. Claiming it was
my fault, because I should have
thrown it out the window, like a
real man does. That's the problem
when you bang a woman who is
house proud, they get all
emotional when you make a tiny
little mess.

Cup Run

Brompton drew a home game for the next round of the cup which was good news because it was against Worksop. That would have meant getting two buses if we had to travel to their ground. But this way it meant we could have a few beers in the Cockerel before the game. I liked the cup because it meant we played teams we wouldn't normally, it also gave the town a positive lift. Well, it did until we would get knocked out then it would be back to thinking we lived in a shit town.

To be fair I didn't know much about Worksop. I knew it was in Nottinghamshire, only because Shabba told me. He only knew it because it was in the Quiz a few weeks ago and he answered Wales. But to be fair to Shabba Geography wasn't his strong point, neither was maths, history science or English. He did though leave school with a qualification in Woodwork. He also got an NVQ in woodwork when his probation officer got him on a training course. Anyway, we both knew Worksop was in Nottinghamshire and you had to get the 22x, then change at Rotherham and get the 19, a right old chore. It was one reason I didn't fancy a replay.

We decided on a plan for the day we would to go to the bus station, hang around and jump their firm when they got in. Take them by surprise, then few beers in town before the game

The night before the game Kenny
the local urban pharmaceutical
rep was in in Cockerel. He sold
Shabba some gear to enhance his
performance and increase his
stamina for the fight with the
Worksop boys.

We had a steady night in the
Cock, like a boxer before a big
fight I abstained from sex,
mainly because Debbie had made it
perfectly clear that our night of
passion was definitely a one off
and Fat Karen had already copped
off with some bloke.

Fat Karen was a popular girl and
most men's back up at last orders
if they hadn't already pulled
that night. On this night, Big
Jock had steamed in, his missus

was in a mood with him so he
needed a backup. He bought Fat
Karen a Tia Maria and diet coke.
I didn't stand a chance after
that. Also, apparently Frank went
down on the women like a man
licking gravy off a plate, so she
knew she was in for a good night.

We met up the next morning at
Shirley's Café, a typical greasy
café for a full English pre fight
meal. All except Mental, he had
something called a vegetarian
breakfast, with added bacon,
sausage and a side order of
chips. His missus was after
another child so he was put on a
strict diet to help his sperm
count, which according to rumour
was extremely low, due to years
of steroid abuse and owning a BMX
when he was a child. I would have

taken the piss out of Mental, if it were not for the years of steroid abuse and he was holding a knife and a folk.

Shabba went into the toilet and took his performance enhancing powder, I finished my cup of tea and we set off to the bus station. We got to platform two and discreetly stood around waiting for the bus to arrive. Mental was well up for it, pacing up and down. He was punching the wall and slapping himself around the face.

Eventually the bus turned up and only three old ladies got off, I asked the driver if any football fans had been on the bus, to which he replied, "yeah, they got

off at the ground, dick head." We
hadn't actually planned for that
and it sort of ruined our mood.

So, we headed for the ground.
Shabba kept complaining, saying
he had to go home. Apparently,
the powder he had been given was
crushed Viagra. He was walking
around with a boner, shame no one
noticed. We couldn't have one of
the firm going into battle with
an erection, but we couldn't send
him on his way.

At the ground we took our place
on the Kop. It was a decent turn
out, Worksop brought ten fans.
There must have been two hundred
in the ground in total it was
madness.

The game itself was uneventful, Brompton won four nil. Big Nige our centre forward and tyre fitter at *Right Said Tread* scored three goals. Their defender scored an own goal, best goal of the day to be fair to him. After the game we waited around near the bus stop for their firm to arrive. After ten minutes stood in the rain they arrived. Mental Nicky just ran at them, screaming like a psycho as he launched into them. I immediately followed. I squared up to this wimpy looking kid. I threw a massive punch at him, shame I missed, cus I reckon it would have really hurt if it connected

Turns out he was a kick boxer, he twated the shit out of me, he didn't even break into a sweat, the cheeky twat. To add insult to injury he also nicked my trainers, I had to walk home bare foot with a bloody nose. How were we meant to know that four of their lads were martial art experts on a day out? Mental got a right old kicking. The only one not to get a kicking was Shabba, they saw his erection and thought he was some pervert getting off on being beat up, into some gay beat up fetish or something. So, he got away unhurt he did however black out on the way home, turns out his three-hour boner caused his blood pressure to drop dangerously low. Would have been a right chore closing the coffin lid had he died.

That evening after I had been home, I got cleaned up and dug out some trainers, I went to the Blue Lion. I met up with Mental and sat around waiting for the draw for the next round of the cup. We spoke about the fight earlier Mental chalked it up as a win, on the grounds that they walked away. Granted the only walked away because we were all laid out on the pavement bleeding, however they walked away so win for BLT.

We later went to the Cock, Naomi the landlord was in a foul mood. Apparently Shabba had been in the toilets for over an hour spanking the monkey. She wasn't concerned with the masturbation, but he had only bought half a lager. Turns out the Glorious Cockerel has a minimum drink limit for flicking one off the wrist.

Shabba later joined us at the bar, his face was red raw and his right arm was dead. Good old Shabba bought a round and he bought Naomi a double so she turned a blind eye to his personal carnal craving earlier.

The night was repetitively a quiet one. Mental spent most of it with his wife. She turned up in a new overly tight-fitting red number. The puppies were well and truly on display, all except their noses. Shabba had copped off with Fat Karen.

I liked Fat Karen, cracking personality, but hey all chubsters do. According to Shabba being with Fat Karen was like opening the window and fucking the night, in her defence seven kids are bound to challenge and stretch the best of muffs.

I got turned down by Debbie and No Morals Sally. To be fair No Morals didn't turn me down, I offered her a drink and she replied "fuck off limp dick." So, I took that as a no, how was I to know she was pre-menstrual? I also lost twenty pounds on the fruit machine. All in all, a shit night, except the kebab on the way home, Greek Sharon gave me extra chips with my pizza order, every cloud and that. I would slip Greek Sharon a length but the stench of chip fat sort of put me off, so did her moustache if I'm being really honest.

THE GLORIOUS COCKEREL

This coming Saturday

THE GLORIIOUS COCKEREL

DRESS UP AND DRINK UP MAYBE GET KNOCKED UP!

'DISCO DANNY'S' DISCO

Hooligans Rampage

By JANET ECCLESTONE

The Glorious Cockerel was last night destroyed after rival football gangs attacked each other. Members of the Bropmton Life Takers were involved in a scuffle that led to over £5,000 of damage. Naomi Doyle (42) said. "This is a lovely, family pub, but last night some feckers came in and all hell broke loose." One person sustained a minor ankle injury. Police said they can't be arsed looking for witnesses

ti
be
or
m
U:
ve
to
ag
co
T
he
th
m
pa
ex
of
m
to
ex
go
lia
in
ti
cr
ar
re
bu
tr

Boys will be Boys

By JANET ECCLESTONE

Wanna be football hooligans from the so called Brompton Life Takers (BLT). Today caused tens of pounds of damage as they kicked over a bin in the town centre. Mrs J Williams (42) said, Some lads were giving it the big I am, one of them kicked the bin over creating a right pissing mess. A spokesperson for AFC Brompton today said. we do not condone anything that the BLT does.

International

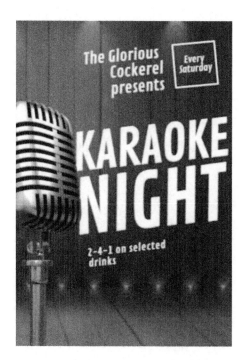

The Glorious Cockerel presents — Every Saturday

KARAOKE NIGHT

2-4-1 on selected drinks

Chow Mein Mao.

9 AM - 1 PM

Opn 7pm till Late
Weekdays and
Weekends

Abra Kebabra BURGER

CHEF'S SPECIAL SAUCE

Blooming Idiots

By JANET ECCLESTONE

A local garden centre was recovering today after football hooligans rampaged and caused over £7 worth of damage. Members of the Brompton Life Takers (BLT) stormed through the garden centre after being involved in a street fight with a rival gang from King Lynn. A spokesperson from the Trimmed Bush said "some kids ran through here and kicked over some plants. Bloody hooligans, I blame the parents myself. It wouldn't happen in my day."

Home Shirt: the famous all Greys

Away Shirt: the famous Black and Grey Hoops

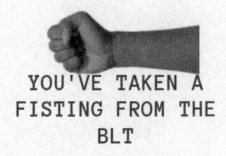

YOU'VE TAKEN A
FISTING FROM THE
BLT

Brompton Life Takers

YOU'VE JUST HAD A
TASTE OF THE BLT

Brompton Life Takers

The Glorious Cockerel

PRESENTS

HAPPY HOUR

FRIDAY NIGHT
AT 8:00PM-9:00PM

233 Boycott Lane
Brompton

The Glorious Cockerel

Beaver House Brewery

The Glorious Cockerel

The Glorious Cockerel

LADIES' NIGHT OUT!

DRESS UP AND DRINK UP
MAYBE GET KNOCKED UP!

This evening Saturday

The Glorious Cockerel

Sunday
Funday

Every Sunday
From 5:00 – 11pm

Cheap Drinks
Disco

On the Pull

The Firm was getting a bit of a
name for itself, especially
around town. I had taken a couple
of muffs as a direct result of
being a hooligan but nothing I
would call regular. The nearest I
had gotten to a long-term shag
was Debbie, and by that, I mean I
banged her once and a week later
she kicked me in the balls when
she overheard me call her a fat
munter down at the Glorious
Cockerel. I know a gentleman
shouldn't talk like that about a
woman but in my defence, she is a
right fat munter.

All the lads were bunked up. Nicky had Shaniqua. Big Jock had Eileen and if she threw him out Fat Karen. Shabba Frank had Mary Hopkins. Beautiful old girl only 74 years young but apparently banged like a sixty-year-old.

Don't get me wrong. I slipped Debbie a length and she was grateful but a meaningful one nighter is all well and good but a man has needs. Who was going to make me a drink in the morning? Or cook me a fry up? Who would help me out when I was tired but horny, and I didn't have the energy for a crafty Tommy Tank? You know the important things like that, stuff to be fair chicks like doing.

Mental kept trying to take the
piss of me, he would often tell
me even Hitler had a girlfriend.
Which to be fair was true, and
made me feel crap about myself.

The world's most evil dictator
had a bird, and I was single? But
mental found it funny

Some tried taking the piss saying
I was ugly, had zero personality,
things like that, harmless banter
amongst mates. All my mates kept
saying there were more fish in
the sea, etc. So I thought time
to get me tackle out, see what
bites. I got dressed in my finest
hooligan gear and headed for the
Blue Lion.

Inside it was mental, Wednesday night 2 for 1 on all cider, lager and stout. The birds were all dressed up in their finest and shortest kit. Lucy swallows was bending over the pool table when I walked in, bloody hell her thong was right up her hoop, I got I right view. If I could lip read, I would have had a field day. It looked like she was smuggling pac man

I went to the bar and got myself a cider and a Guinness chaser. Whilst I'm there this little lad is giving it the big I am to some tarts. I looked at him and thought to myself 'what a twat' mainly because he looked a real twat. He was throwing his money around like he was some rock n roll star, the birds were hanging all over him.

I went to the pool table and put my pound on the side. I don't usually play pool but I thought I would give it a go and give Lucy some of my chat up lines.

Big mistake, Lucy didn't laugh once at any of my lines and she spanked me royally at pool. There I was pouring out my lines and nothing. I decided, enough was enough and I hit her with the big lines, the ones guaranteed to knock any chick sideways I went straight up to her, looked her bang in the eyes and said to her, 'Lucy, phone your mam tell her you've pulled'. Boom. Well, Lucy welled up a bit and shouts at me

in that screechy voice chicks
have 'you sick bastard you know
my mom died last week.' Well, I
honestly forgot, I felt a right
tool I can tell you. To be fair,
it was a week ago. So, I thought
I would you know make her laugh
make her forget her problems. The
ladies like a man with a cracking
sense of humour. I said 'Lucy
have you got pet insurance.' Lucy
lost it big time, even more than
when I mentioned her dead mother.
I was going to reply 'because I
am going to destroy your pussy'.
But Lucy jumps at me screaming
'You know we had Tyson put down
after he bit my mother and
severed her artery.' I haven't
seen a woman that mad in a long
time, not since the day I lost my
virginity. I was that excited to
see boobs I shot me muck

instantly, my girlfriend back she then went mental, mainly because I was looking at a picture of her mom at the time, and her mom was my step mother, awkward. I decided at that point to leave Lucy to grieve the loss of her mom and her faithful family dog Tyson, grief is a funny old thing. Lucy was red with rage screaming some shit at me being insensitive or something. Chicks, when they are premenstrual they can be well moody.

I was about to leave when the bloke at the bar, giving loads to the chicks looks at me and says 'what.' I thought to myself 'oh yeah big boy.' That was it game on I couldn't let some geezer take the liberty out of me, not on my home soil.

I waited for the gobshite to go
to the toilets, then I would
follow him in and give him a
right kicking. Within minutes, he
put his pint down and walks to
the Gents. I turned and followed
him in. As soon as we walked in
the door, I pushed him and he
slipped on all the piss, he went
flying across the toilets and
smashed his head on the urinals.
Out cold her went.

I walked out, shook the piss off
my Adidas Gazelles and went to
the bar to finish my drink.
Within minutes the place is going
barmy. Limp Wrist Gary was
looking through the glory hole
and he sees Deaf Mike sparked out
on the floor. He goes to tell the
landlord and calls an ambulance.
Everyone is going mental as Deaf

Mike was a local legend. He lost some of his hearing in a sponsored charity thing for kids and that.

Deaf Mick was the local's favourite, he once shook hands with Princess Michael of Kent and made the local news. Many years ago, Deaf Mike tried to jump over 10 shopping trolleys on his push bike to raise money for kids' charity, unfortunately for him as he took off. Lanky Keith set of the pyrotechnics. Well, I say pyrotechnics it was a couple of air bombs strapped together, they went off right next to Mikes face, blew out his eardrums, scared him for life; he broke his leg as he landed on the second shopping trolley, and he also ripped off of his testicles. He got disability for loosing the hearing in one ear, so a nice result for him.

Anyway, turns out he wasn't saying 'what' to me, he was saying it to Maureen the barmaid. I got the wrong end of the story and well incidentally, he went diving head first into the urinal. I of course said nothing and just left the place and headed to the Cock.

Soon as I got to the Cock, word was out Deaf Mike had been assaulted. I played dumb and said nothing. Mental was doing his usual saying he was going to kill someone. He really lost it when he eventually heard about Deaf Mike. I was starting

to get a little annoyed so
Michael Hunt had raised a few
quid for a kid's charity. It
was strange, I once did a
charity run, you don't hear me
bleat on about it.

I was raising money for the local
children's' hospital, I decided
to dress as He Man, you know
something for the kids and that.
Anyway, on the day I got there
and it was freezing so I put my
knock off tracksuit on. It turns
out with the tracksuit and blonde
wig it made me look like Jimmy
Saville. I got chased through
town by Nonce Sense, the local
paedo hunters. They kicked seven
shades of shit out of me when
they caught me. Come on I ask how
many people would do a charity
marathon dressed as Jimmy Saville

to raise money for children? To
be fair though I did raise
£17.20.

Locals felt sorry for Deaf Mick,
and he raised over two grand, as
well as gaining local celebrity
status. I got a kicking for £17.
No justice.

Anyway, I'm at the bar keeping
myself quiet, got a drink and
tried to see if I could finger
bang Nasty Helen at the end of
the night. To be fair things were
going well, Helen was slightly
juiced up, she was giggling to
all my jokes and bants. Was
turning into a decent night

Unfortunately, things went a bit
pear shaped when Naomi took a
phone call off the Blue Lion,
there CCTV system, set up by Limp
Wrist Gary for some reason
covered the gents' toilets. I
could be clearly seen pushing
Deaf Mike before his head landed
in the urinal. Naomi pointed out
it was probably and accident as
the toilet floor was always
covered in piss. Both Landlords
agreed, and between them agreed I
should take a simple slap for my
faux pas, and all would be
forgiven.

Unfortunately for me Naomi was
the one that gave me the gentle
slap, knocked me out cold for six
minutes. When I came round Nasty
Hellen slapped me for pushing her
deaf brother into the urinals.

Before Naomi slapped me again for drinking in a rivals pub.

I went home that night with two black eyes, concussion, piss on my Adidas Gazelles and a semi, as Nasty Helen pissed off with Luke Postlethwaite, the dwarf got to finger her instead of me. Have to admit not my best night out, however, not my worst.

Game Day

So Brompton are playing at home against a local-ish team in the league. Myself, Mental, Shabba and Col are in the Glorious Cockerel having a few drinks and the usual banter. We were getting ourselves ready to go to the game when in walks plod. Our local police officer WPC Blake, decent girl, if she wasn't police officer, she would be the sort of chick you'd go for. She walked over to Naomi and the two of them had a chat. As they are chatting WPC Blake keeps looking over at us.

Nothing new there, as a hooligan the police usually give you a bit of a hard time. Anyway, after a few minutes of chatting WPC Blake turns

gestures to us that we are wankers
and walks out the bar. Naomi came
over and told us that WPC Blake was
in a mood because her bosses were
giving her a hard time about the
local chavs and vandalism etc.

She had also mentioned that
Helmsley AFC were coming into town
with a coach full of supporters.
This was like audio pornography to
Mental. He suddenly sprung to life,
he's bouncing around, getting all
excited for the violence.

Naomi went mental at us, she
informed us that the coach was
heading to the Glorious Cockerel,
and under no circumstances was
there to be any trouble, as she was
serving beers and lunch and a new
higher price to make a killing from

our visitors. Naomi politely and in a way that left us in no doubt informed us that any trouble would result in A: us being barred from the bar, and B: she would take it as a personal insult to herself. Which basically meant we'd get a kicking.

Well Mental, wasn't happy a all, but even a psycho like him wouldn't mess with Naomi so he calmed down a little.

About ten minutes later the coach arrived and Naomi welcomed over thirty visiting football fans. Naomi had banged the price of lager up by a pound and her all day breakfast, served 12 - 3 was raised by £1.50.

All was going well until one of the
Helmsley lads whilst leaving the
pub casually mentioned to his mate
that the lager tasted like piss.
Well Naomi took this as a personal
insult and came round the bar and
chased the lad outside. Mental went
diving in and all hell broke loose.

There we were outside the pub
brawling with the Hemsley boys. WPC
Blake and some of her mates were
outside in the van. They sat there
for a while and eventually came
over and broke up the fight. Naomi
dragged Col back into the pub and
slammed the doors shut. Myself and
Shabba and Mental picked ourselves
off the floor. WPC Blake didn't
arrest any of us. She said the
beating we took from five elderly
gentlemen was punishment enough. To

add insult to injury the police
just stood there laughing. Wankers.

We brushed ourselves down and
limped to the game, Brompton lost
three nil.

Got Myself a Bird

One dull rainy Friday morning I
was walking down the high street,
minding my own business. Who is
walking towards me, only Badger.
Badger was an old mate I knew
from school, he was the kind of
kid in school that wasn't really
a trouble causer, higher
spirited. The sort of kid that
would stick a new kid head in the
toilet for a laugh, nothing too
serious like. He would get fixed
term excluded for minor things
like swearing at a teacher, or
slashing the head teachers'
tyres. You know mindless,
harmless fun. Anyway, we stopped
and chatted, he explained that

after his minor two-year prison stretch, driving without insurance, without a licence and taking without owners' consent, he was going straight, his mom had forgiven him for taking and writing off her car. He'd got his own business, landscape gardening. Business wasn't going to well, based on urban council estates not having gardens, and Badger knowing nothing about plants, oh and the economy. So, he sold his shovel and liquidated his firm. We had a good natter and I told him to meet me later that day in the Cock and Beaver for a few Lagers.

That evening I went to the Cock, my mate Badger was already there. He was casually dressed in the style usually associated with a homeless beggar. There's me in a knock of Armani jumper, smart jeans and some new Nike trainers. But credit to him he had received his Unemployment payment, so he got the beers in.

We got chatting and I explained about the firm. He was well up for it. I explained there was an initiation process and he wasn't arsed, anything for a giggle that lad. So, we settled in at the bar and got a few beers in us.

Mental called in around nine o'clock, just in time for the Wheels of Steel disco bonanza. That's when the DJ bangs on some old school rock classics and the punters go a little mental on the dance floor. Between us we decided Badger's induction into the firm would be that he had to give Naomi a good squeeze on her arse. Badger was well up for it as he put it, "she's well fit and definitely up for it." So, there he goes, walks straight up to Naomi, who is at the end of the bar, without hesitations he slaps her straight on the rump and says "so love." That's as far as he got, Naomi swung round and without missing a beat punches Badger square on the jaw. He went down quicker than a cut price prostitute. Bang. He's out on the floor, Naomi starts kicking seven shades out of him. She is screaming at him like a woman possessed. Me and Mental were pissing ourselves laughing as his limp body is being kicked around the pub.

Old Naomi is only a skinny thing, size eight. But what a fighter. She's screaming stuff at Badger, and slapping him like you would a ginger step child. Luckily Naomi's fella was there, he grabs Naomi and pulls her away. She's still trying to kick old Badger as she is being pulled away. Col dragged her away to a safe distance to calm her down. Badger eventually got up went to the toilet to clean himself up. One broken nose and a life time acceptance to the Brompton Life Takers was the result of his quest.

Badger and Naomi squared things up later on, he explained that it was a test, after he, myself and Mental had bought her a few drinks she calmed down. Col was in a good mood though. Turns out after a barny, old Naomi is rather aroused sexually, and he gets a bunk up and breakfast in bed. So, everyone was a winner really.

That night about 11:30 the disco was coming to an end; the erection section had started. The part of the night when the slower songs come on and you get to bag one of the girls that hasn't already pulled. Badger was on the dance floor, arms most of the way around Big Helen smooching to Carless Whisper. I clocked Edda stood by the bar. She was a classy girl, spoke well had a job, she was a receptionist at *For Eyes*, the local opticians.

She had an arse so high and tight, and tits where God originally put them. She didn't have any kids or ex boyfriends, to be fair she had a reputation for being stuck up and frigid. Turns out she was quiet and shy, apparently there is a difference. She was a classy bird. The sort you'd finger and not just on a first date.

She was stood near the bar drinking a baileys and lemonade, and wearing what I can only describe as a dress that looked like she had painted it on. She was definitely up for it, I could tell; her legs were freshly shaved, always a clear sign.

Her sister had copped off with
some lad earlier and left the
bar, Edda was stood nervously all
alone. I steamed over to her like
a proud stallion on the prowl, I
gave her one of my many chat up
lines. "I was thinking about you
last night." To which she replies
"Why?" Boom. I hit her with the
killer line "I was having a
cheeky wank and needed to get to
the vinegar strokes." She didn't
seem overly impressed, and she
never laughed.

So, I hit her with the big one, I
looked her straight in the eyes,
"I don't usually ask a girl this
until I have got her pregnant,
but, what's your name.' Edda just
looked at me and said "it's me
Edda, I live a few houses away
from you, remember." She didn't

see the humour or exoticness of my chat up line, so I went to plan B, bought her Baileys and Blackcurrant and after a bit of boring polite chat we got on the dance floor for a smooch to Everybody Hurts, beautiful romantic little number. I pulled her close and let my semi rub gently against her so she knew I was interested. Girls love that sort of thing.

As soon as the song ended Naomi shouts time at the bar and on come the lights. This usually is a bad thing, seeing the sort you've ended up with, it can easily sober a man up, however on this occasion wow, what a result. Edda was by far the prettiest girl in the bar, and the only one with all her original teeth.

Naomi was screaming like a Dublin banshee trying to get everyone out of the bar. She had that glint in her eye. Old Col was in for a night of loving, whether he wanted it or not. I took Edda for a pizza down at *Finger Lickers*. Before taking her to my place for a bit of fun.

Back at mine things didn't go according to plan. Edda was a cracking lass. Sense of humour needed working on though. I tried to light a fart, she didn't even snigger. We had a little kiss but she wouldn't let me grope her. Turns out she won't let a man bone her for at least half a dozen dates, the slag. She wont even let a man feed the pony.

Turns out no bloke had gone passed two dates with her, as the men our way get bored if a lass doesn't put out first night. Probably the only woman I had ever met that didn't put out on the first hook up, I sort of respected her for that, even though I had a full-on boner.

Despite my absolute ragging hard on, I accepted defeat. We kissed and cuddled for a while, no tongues, Edda insisted.

We even shared a bed that night but nothing happened. I waited until Edda fell asleep, then I took her thong to the bathroom and had a few cheeky sniffs whilst I cracked one out. So, not a complete waste of a night.

The next morning Edda woke me
wearing one of my old I Kissed
the Blarney Stone T-shirts and a
cute smile, a cup of tea. Her
cute smile turned into a strange
look when she saw her thong stook
to my face, but she wasn't overly
offended. She climbed into bed
next to me and we chatted for a
while and at that moment I did
her the honour of asking her to
be my lass, you know official
like. She smiled and said "Yea I
don't see why not." Result! Daz
has a bird! It was so romantic.

I walked her back to her flat
that morning. Her dad was there.
Edda said something in German and
he gave me a hug and said welcome
to the family. Then invited me in
to his family home.

His house was amazing, he had a lovely warm welcoming place. His Iron Cross proudly sitting in a frame on the wall. Pictures everywhere of his girls and some of him during the war, looking dejected after El Alamein. Photos of Doris in her younger days working in the NAFFI, she was a decent bird back then.

Doris made me a cracking full English and we sat around chatting. To be honest it was a nice morning if not a strange one. Never known a family to sit and eat together, never mind get on. Her father was happy that Edda a boyfriend apparently, he had spent years thinking she was lesbian or frigid, or worse, both.

I left after a while, Edda gave me a cracking goodbye kiss, this time she slipped a bit of tongue in. Well, we were officially dating now so she had to up her game a little. I left with a spring in my step and a semi in my pants. Shame I had to go to shopping for my mom.

The rest of the day I hung around my flat, had a shower, a shave and a shit. I spent the rest of the day watching TV and waiting impatiently for night to fall so I could go down the Cockerel and Beaver with my girlfriend. The regulars would be well jealous when they saw a top boy walk in with a decent bit of skirt on his arms.

When the evening finally arrived, I put on my new aftershave, Shart pour Homme. Burglar Bill got it for me, apparently it is a hint of apricot and cedar, all I knew is it burnt my face and smelt like toilet duck. I put on a sweatshirt, clean jeans and a pair of adidas Gazelle. I looked top draw. I walked down to Edda's and had a quick chat with her dad, because Edda was running thirty minutes later. Chicks hey.

When she arrived, she looked amazing, her blonde hair was perfect her make up, wasn't to heavy handed. She had on some leatherette leggings and a jumper that said 'Heiß' which is some foreign for Hot, she looked so cool. That's what I liked about her, pure class. European with a

British sense of irony, hard to find in an ordinary chick.

We went to the Blue Lion for a livener and for me to show Edda off to my mom. I had a pint of lager top, Edda had a Guinness and black, because well, she is a sophisticated lady. Mom took a shine to Edda immediately, once she believed me that I hadn't paid for her, they got on really well. Unfortunately, Debbie was in and her and Edda didn't get on. Debbie always thought Edda was a 'frigid slag.' And Edda thought Debbie was just 'a slag'.

After a swift couple we left there and went to the Cock, once we arrived, I palmed Edda off with Shaniqua and No Morals, whilst me and the boys had a few beers and a talk about the next game. Girls love that sort of thing, being left alone to talk make-up and shopping, whilst the men crack on about football and violence. It's a genetic thing.

Col was behind the bar, he had a bit of a limp, old Naomi had destroyed him the night before, but he wasn't complaining, well to be fair he was complaining, about the soreness, not the ride. Badger was in, he was on his best behaviour though as Naomi had warned him off, in her charming Gaelic way. The night was going well, and the lagers were flowing nicely. Towards the end of the night some lads came in, they were on a stag night from Rotherham. One of the lads made a

comment about Shaniqua's tits. To
be fair they were hanging out,
well for her they were covered
up, for any normal lass they were
hanging out. However as per
normal Mental lost it. So, Mental
and Badger steamed into them, I
was a little behind them because
I slipped on the dance floor and
really hurt my ankle.

All hell broke loose. There were
bottles being thrown, punches
flying everywhere. I headbutted
one lad, to be honest it didn't
do much damage as he was wearing
a baseball cap at the time. The
peak of the cap just bounced off
me. So, I waded in, threw about
fifteen punches, a couple even
landed, didn't half hurt my hands
like. We eventually ran the boys
out of that pub, well, the firm

did, helped by most of the women in the bar. I managed to punch another one of them on his back as he ran out.

Chairs were suddenly being smashed by Naomi. She shouted at us to join in as she was going to stick in an insurance claim.

Pint glasses were shattered, chairs and tables smashed to pieces. Eileen smashed a framed picture of Red Rum over Big Jocks head. She later admitted she got a little carried away.

That night BLT looked really tasty. The headline a few days later in the Brompton Gazette read 'Tossers smash up pub.' I

still have that cut out in my
scrap book.

The police arrived later and shut
the pub down due to the amount of
damage. It looked like a bloody
war zone. I limped home with
Edda, my ankle was giving me some
hassle. When we got back to mine,
she put some ice on my ankle and
made me a hot chocolate drink to
ease the pain. That night we went
to bed, still only cuddling was
allowed, but I got to see her
tits as she climbed into bed, so
result. To be fair I was in that
much pain, I probably would have
only been firing on half me usual
cylinders.

The next morning, I woke, Edda
was fast asleep. I laid there

thinking how lucky I was, and how
with me on my back and aroused
the covers looked like I was in a
tent.

Arrested Development

Brompton were playing in the next round of the cup. It was a dull cold wet morning. To be fair it was always dull and cold, after all I lived in Yorkshire. I was up early, showered and ready to go. Edda had made me a packed lunch for the trip, Corned beef and mint sauce sandwiches, she wasn't a great cook, but do you have to be a good cook if you look as hot as she did?

Mental was on the phone early; he was well up for a mad one. Badger was all excited. Mongoose and Shabba were in the Cock by 11.01 having a livener, to get in the mood.

The Firm was heading for Gainsborough. We set off around 12 noon and got a through bus to their town centre. All the way there Mental was getting himself wound up. His plan was simple find a pub, smash it up and let everyone know a top firm was in town. We got to town relatively early. We found a decent looking pub, the George and Dragon. As we walked in the landlady came over and said "Good Morning lads." Boom, straight away Badger pipes up "Alright love where's George." That was it, barred from the pub. Turns out not all fat ugly women have a good personality.

We walked down to the next place the Squirrel. As we walked in Mental ran straight up to the bar jumps over and tries to headbutt

the barman, he missed by about
three feet and smashed himself
straight flat on the floor. I
picked up an ashtray and through
it behind the bar. Next thing
landlord appears with two huge
German Shepard's, never ran so
fast out of a place. We bolted
down the road. Half way down we
realised Mental wasn't there so
we sat on a wall and waited for
him to catch up. Mainly because
we were knackered from the run.

Before you can say 'you're
nicked' a police car arrives and
we were all arrested. We were all
taken to the local station and
banged up. Well, all except
Mental he was taken to hospital
with bite injuries to his arse
and legs. The German Shepard's
had a right time on him. After

about an hour or so in the nick
we were released, all charged
with Public Order. Except Badger
he was held in custody, he was
wanted in Lincolnshire for a
Fraud and other related chargers.
Turns out his gardening business
was a way of scamming money out
of people. He got four years for
it.

We were told by the Police to
leave the area or else, so we did
what we wanted to do, and we left
the area.

When we got back word was out
that one of the boys was in
hospital and we had been
arrested. The girls in the Cock
were well up for us that night.

Edda came into the bar, all
dressed up and looking glam, in a
tight-fitting dress. Half way
down her first pint she whispered
in my ear that she had developed
feelings for me and we should
take the relationship to the next
level. I was now allowed to enter
the promised land, by that she
meant her snatch.

We had a right giggle all night,
danced a bit, drank a bit, I got
the DJ to play Ninety-Nine Red
Balloons, as I know the Germans
love that tune. It's like the
national anthem to them. Edda
dragged me on the dance floor and
we partied for a while. Then we
had a top-notch smooch during the
erection section. Disco Danny
played all the classics, Careless
Whisper. Can't Help Falling in

Love - Elvis. She Makes my Day -
Robert Palmer. Then boom. I'm
Gonna Be (500 Miles) - The
Proclaimers, the place went
mental, perfect, always finish on
a high.

On the way home we smashed a
kebab and a portion of fries,
with onion rings down at *Abra
Kebabra*. Then straight back to
mine and to bed where Edda
finally allowed us to take our
relationship to a physical level.

Within minutes I was riding her
like a cowboy. The best thing
about sleeping with a woman of
limited experience or in Edda
case zero experience. One, she
doesn't know if I'm good or bad
at it. Two, her secret garden is

nice and tight, like the time I
stuck my penis in a vice for a
laugh in GCSE metalwork class.

She was freshly waxed downstairs,
it was so smooth, I slipped off
her a few times.

I had drunk a fair few beers
earlier so my performance was of
the extended variety, Edda's
introduction to sex was a long
and enjoyable one, the lucky moo.

The next morning, I woke up with
a right headache. 8 pints of
lager top and a kebab will do
that to the best of them. Edda
was lying next to me all womanly
and angelic. Well except when she
dropped her guts. Rancid it was,

almost burnt my nostrils and so
dense I could have knitted it. It
was a mixture of kebab, Guinness
and a sauerkraut odour but Edda
looked so innocent and cute
snuggled up asleep, after wafting
the duvet I snuggled up and gave
her a cuddle. My semi
romantically, and gently stabbing
her in the back, chicks love that
sort of thing in a morning.

Down South

Our first visit down south was finally here. The Brompton Life Takers were heading to the capital. Brompton versus Saint Albans. I'd been looking forward to this game for months. BLT down the capital. The Chelsea head-hunters were away to Villa. West Hams ICF were at Southampton. The only serious firm stopping us from taking over London was Tottenham's Yid Army.

I was awake at silly o clock, nervous, excited and horny. This was a big day for the boys. Mental had arranged all the travel details. Shabba was well up for it. Big Jock had spent the previous night sat in with a

take-away to get Eileen all
moist, putting her in a good
mood. Eileen would do almost
anything for a mixed kebab, large
fries and a diet coke.

Edda, was awake and dressed for
work, she gave me a kiss and told
me to be careful. Bless, chicks
are sensitive creatures. I
promised her I would be good, and
back in time to take her to the
local curry house 'Singh for your
supper', for a curry later that
night. I set off and met the boys
at the bus stop, we got on the
bus and headed for Sheffield.

Once there we nipped across from
the bus station to the train
station. Word must have got out
we were in town, South Yorkshire

Police everywhere. So, we put our heads down and walked to the platform. On the opposite platform were about 90 Sheffield United boys. Mental decided to give them some abuse, started chanting about giving them a kicking. They were chanting BBC (*Blades Business Crew*) so we started chanting ITV at them; it was so funny. However, it sort of backfired, twenty of their boys darted over the platforms and we went toe to toe with them. We got absolutely leathered. I was punched in the head by four different blokes in the space of about twenty seconds. Luckily the police were on it. Some of their boys were arrested. Shabba was taken to hospital with a smashed-up face. We tried to explain to the paramedic that he always

looked like that but they
wouldn't have any of it. Within
moments the train arrived and we
jumped on. Giving the wanker sign
to the United fans on the next
platform.

It was around about the time the
train went past Derby that Mental
looked at the fixture list and we
realised we were in fact at home
to Neston. The Saint Albans game
was the following week. We also
discovered from a commuter that
Saint Albans is its own place and
not inside London. It was turning
out to be a bit of a chore.

Even though we were frustrated at
Mentals ability to read or in
this case not read. We decided to

stay on the train, go to London
and have a decent day out. Maybe
go to Buckingham Palace to see
HM.

The first thing I noticed when I
got to London was that the
streets were in fact paved with
gold. However, unfortunately the
gold was piss. Turns out London
is a dump. Also why build a
palace for the Queen so far away
from the train station? We had to
take the underground, which is a
horrible experience. Everyone
looks miserable on the tube, and
I said hello to this young lass.
The look she gave me, you'd have
thought I asked to shit on her
chest. Also why are all the
prices so bloody expensive?

We went down St James's Palace
and tormented the guards on duty,
it was hilarious. Turns out
though that they can move,
especially if you touch them. Old
Mental almost had a bayonet stuck
up his hoop.

We then went to Green Park and
threw some stones at hippies and
hipsters. Before going to Soho.

In Soho we lost Big Jock, me and
Mental was walking around, trying
not to catch the eyes of the gays
and Jock vanished. Turned around
Big Jock is nowhere to be seen,
it later transpired he nipped
into a gay bar for a piss. Being
the good mates, we are we left
him. Be a right laugh old Jock
walking around Soho looking for

us, whilst were on the train back up north.

On the way back we got on the train with some boys from Coventry. They were alright to be honest good banter, well would have been if we could understand them, apparently what they were speaking was English, just not the sort and normal bloke could recognise. When they got off a Leicester Mental tripped one of them up, then slammed the train door shut, as the train pulled away, we gave them the wanker sign. Result another firm we'd seen off.

Back in the Cock we were telling everyone about our day, how we took two firms on. Eileen came in

going absolutely crazy, Jock had
phoned he was at a bloke's house
called Raul, they'd met in Soho.
He wasn't coming back until the
morning.

Edda was in the bar with No
Morals and Eva. Eva was in a foul
mood; she'd met this new man.
Apparently, he'd stood her up
because his wife wanted to have a
night in. Eva was not happy, she
was going to dump him, but they
had a weekend to Blackpool booked
so she gave him a second chance.

I was so tired; I only had a few
beers before heading home. Edda
arrived back about an hour after
me. Disco Danny had come on to
her and she wasn't happy. I went
crazy, I took my dressing gown
off and quickly popped on some

clothes. Unfortunately, in the rush that I was in, I put on Edda thong instead of my boxers. Edda didn't want me to get arrested and was really worried about me, I gave her a peck on the cheek and said "Don't worry babe." Before steaming out, down the estate and into the Cock. The run down there was awkward, Edda's thong was right up my hoop. I had a right limp by the time I got to the cock. Mental could see I was in a mood. I told him what had happened and before I could say anything he'd dived at Danny and started smashing him up. I of course joined in, after I pulled the thong out me cheeks. We gave him a right good whack.

Naomi came over and broke the fight up, I told her what he'd

done, she gave Danny a right
crack. He went out cold. She told
me and Mental to 'feck off.' So,
we took her advice and left.

I got back to the flat and told
Edda what had happened, before I
could finish, I was conkers deep
in her silk axe wound. The knight
in shining armour routine really
made her juice up. Afterwards,
she even made me a cup of tea,
without me asking her. That girl
was in a good mood, despite her
favourite thong being ruined for
ever. I pointed out it wasn't
ruined, skid marks wash out, Edda
wasn't having it and threw them
in the bin.

The next day Danny phoned me and
explained that he was drunk and
didn't mean it, he was trying to

bag Eva. He told me he fancies
Eva like mad, and finds Edda
plain, boring and uninteresting.
We sorted it out and the next
time I saw him he bought me a
pint. So, friends again.

Jock arrived back from London
four days later, he couldn't
remember much of his time there.
Except he apparently had a blast,
saw some queens and made some
good friends. He was planning to
go down again and meet Raul for
Pride.

Blackpool on tour

The season was going well, Brompton had made a cracking start, the cup run was going well and I had a bird. Nothing could stop BLT now.

Down at the new refurbished Glorious Cockerel Naomi was a happy landlord. Her insurance money had come through and the pub was looking smart, well it was looking smarter. Burglar Bill had got a new set of tables and chairs for £100. Which made Naomi happy as the insurance company paid out £5000.

Naomi and Col had got new
matching jewellery and so things
were all happy. Mental was fully
recovered from his dog bites and
all seventeen stitches had been
removed. To him they were a real
battle honour, he would show them
to everyone who asked, and
everyone who didn't ask got to
see them also.

Brompton were down to play Gayton
FC the next game of the season.
Seen as it was near Liverpool, we
decided to take the girls along,
they could have a day shopping
and we could go on the rampage,
then Blackpool for the night and
a few beers, proper romantic
weekend.

We arranged it like a military
operation. Shabba booked a mini

bus, he knew a man who could get his hands on one. Naomi offered to make us all a pack up, at a reasonable price that we couldn't really turn down. The pack up was expensive for half a dozen Spam sandwiches and some crisps, but no one had to bottle to tell Naomi so we placed an order.

On the day we met down at the Cockerel, Me and Edda were first to arrive. Then Shabba turned up looking like a homeless student. Mental and Shaniqua rocked up, which caused a little controversy. See Naomi had on leatherette leggings and a sweatshirt, so did Shaniqua. After a quick discussion it was decided Shaniqua would change into a leatherette mini skirt. It only took Col about ten minutes to calm Naomi down, stroking her hair like she was a puppy. Mongoose and Jock rocked up with Eileen. Then two minutes before the bus was due Debbie, no Morals and Fat Mandy arrived.

Twenty minutes later, Shabba called his mate, turns out he was running late because he had trouble getting the bus. Problem solved after a gentle threat of violence from Naomi, the bus turned up not long after. Unfortunately for the firm Shabba's mate worked for the Varity Club of Great Britain and it was written all over the bus. Made it look like the special school was on a day out. Having fat Mandy starring out of the back window eating a Greggs sausage roll just made matter worse.

We all jumped on after a huge debate of the pros and cons of travelling on a Variety bus, and we set off for the sunny sites of the Wirral. We rocked up at a place called Parkgate only a few hours after we set off. Now Parkgate isn't far from Gayton, however we had to stop as everyone was bursting for a piss. We went into a pub on the front and everyone dashed straight for the toilets. As we came out Col informed us, we were all barred. Turns out the landlord complained about us diving into the toilets, so Naomi accused him of being racist to the paddies and headbutted him. The landlord had made a comment about Naomi being

a gobshite and aggressive so she
showed him that he was in fact
right.

We left Parkgate moments later.
We shot over to the ground,
double speed just in case the pub
had called the police on us. The
girls decided rather than go shop
lifting in Liverpool they would
come to the game. Watching
football with the women was ok,
but not the same. It's like
watching Greek Andy spit roast a
kebab with a vegan.

The game was terrible 0 - 0 each.
There wasn't much banter with the
home fans, they were either
elderly or families. We spent
most of the game chanting BLT,
then the home supporters for some
reason starts chanting Sausage

and Egg at us? Knob heads. The game was so rubbish, that when our players came over to applauded us at the end, Naomi barred two of them from the Glorious Cockerel, for being shite.

At the end of a shite game, we left the ground got back on the Variety bus and headed to Blackpool for a night out. The bed and Breakfast Mental had booked us in was recently awarded one star from the AA which I think was two stars to many. The room me and Edda had was a shitty room with bunkbeds. The on suite was a tiny sink, a shitty mould-stained shower and a toilet that the previous guest didn't flush. The woman who ran it knew Mental as her boy went to the same young offender's institute together, he was currently doing twelve years in a Turkish prison for trying to bring drugs out of the country. As the hostess put it "he was doing them a favour by removing drugs from their shitty country. He's a bloody political prisoner." She had a point if he hadn't been taking the drugs out, there would be more in Turkey for the locals to get smashed on. Makes you think, doesn't it?

Once we had put our bags down, we all met up and went on the arcades in Blackpool. We had a right laugh. I won a teddy bear for Edda on one of those grabby machines, only cost me six quid. They were selling the same bear in the market for one pound fifty. But it's the thrill of the

chase, and Edda's face was so
pretty when she saw me win it,
she gave me that look women give
you when they are going to give
you a blowy.

Col and Naomi were a right laugh
both of them had plastic
policeman's helmets on, they were
walking around twating people
with their plastic truncheons.
And they had the biggest teddy
bear you'd ever seen. Col won it
on a shooting gallery, Naomi was
well chuffed she was definitely
giving Col that blowy look.

We went back to the Bed and
Breakfast, to get changed and get
our blowy's. Problem was Mental
was in the next room to us, his
bathroom backed on to our
bedroom. Listening to him squeeze

one out was definitely not what I wanted to hear as I got to the vinegar stroke.

After we had showered, shaved and in Mental's case had a monumental shit, we met up. Every one of us all dressed in our finest ready for a night on the piss. Even Shabba made the effort, there he was proud as a peacock in his new Vest, well new for him; Oxfam sixty pence, bargain.

Blackpool on a night out is a great time, first pub we went to had karaoke. We had a few beers and banged some tunes out, I sung David Hasselhoff's - Looking for Freedom, Edda being part German should have loved that, turns out she'd never heard of it. As she once explained to me in her gentle tone, "my father is German I was born in Doncaster you prick." Passionate people the Germans. Also, history shows us, you don't annoy them.

Mental did is usual karaoke number, Fire Starter, that song was special to him. He followed it with Smack my Bitch up, romantic, it was the song he sang to Shaniqua at their engagement karaoke. The session finished off with Naomi and Col singing Mel and Kim's Respectable, was a quality start to the evening.

Second pub was ok, until the night took a turn. Some local with a bit of an attitude said hello to Shaniqua as she went to the bar. Mental took offence and a bit of an argument broke out. I

decided to calm it down. So, I
stepped in and had a chat with
Mental and as it is just calming
down the local calls him a
dickhead. I without thinking of
my own personal safety smacks the
kid in the back of the head as he
is walking away. He goes down,
clump, proper hard punch it was.
My hand starts to throb
instantly, but being a proper
lad, I held back the tears, just.

Next thing all his mates arrive
and an almighty ruck breaks out,
the boys of the BLT versus some
locals. By the end of it Naomi
and Col are the only two
standing, Naomi took four out
single handed. There were blue
lights everywhere within minutes.

Edda came over to me a kneeled down, I got a decent view of her baps, next thing I know I'm on a trolley in Accident and Emergency I have a broken hand from punching someone in the back of the head, a broken nose and a black eye, from someone punching me in the front of the head. Mental received a head injury, to be fair he loved it though, and who can spot a head injury on a nutter? Shabba was fuming, her hair extensions had come out in the fighting, Mongoose and Jock both took kicking's to their gentleman's area, Eileen said he couldn't get a stiffy for weeks after. However, he hadn't really got one with Eileen since arriving back from London, probably jet lag. Anyway, police arrested the five lads from the

bar, for public order and
underage drinking.

I spent three days in hospital,
having wires put in my hand as I
broke two bones in three places.
I came out with a massive pot on
my arm. I also had to get the
train back as everyone pissed off
back to Brompton the next day.
The Variety Club needed its mini
bus back.

Ebba was waiting for me when I
got back, she made me a full
English as a welcome home
present, unfortunately everything
was burnt to a cinder. Bless her,
arse of an angel cooking skills
sadly missing.

So, we went to her mams house and we let her mam cook as she cooked like an angel however her arse sadly a lot further south now age had ravaged her. Cracking full English, with sauerkraut, excellent brew and Ebba knew with me having a pot on she'd have to give me a hand with my sexual frustrational needs. So not a bad morning at all.

That evening we went to the Cock for a few beers and the lads and lasses bought me drinks, for being a war hero and abandoning me in Blackpool.

Danny, the owner of the local Chinese 'Chow Mein Mao's' gave me a free portion of prawn toast when we popped in for some snap and Ebba wore some very revealing

underwear in the bedroom when we
arrived back.

It made the original agonising
pain, hand surgery and minor
disfigurement all worth it in the
end.

Stag Do

Turns out whilst I was in hospital having surgery for a broken hand, old Naomi had gotten Colin to give her a surprise wedding proposal. Turns out Naomi's vomiting in the morning was not a result of her being pregnant it was a result of never cleaning the beer lines. She was so relieved she decided that her and Colin should get married, and maybe occasionally clean the beer lines.

Naomi told Colin that I was going to be his best man. I was honoured when he asked me. It turns out he wanted it to be his brother but Naomi hated him, so she picked me.

Now part of being a best man is
arranging the stag do. I spoke
with Edda about it and she told
me to ask her sister Eva to do a
turn on the night, she also
managed to get her sister Eva to
give me a discount on her normal
fees. Eva was a proper business
woman; she ran a mobile catering
service during the day and had a
stable of strippers in the
evening. Her catering business
would supply the food, you know
cold buffet proper nice food for
an engagement and her stable of
exotic dancers would supply
entertainment and additional
extras for a price. Some of the
girls she had working for her
were well classy, some even had
GCSE's.

The day of the stag do was also
the day we played Kidsgrove at
home. So, two for one. We'd go to
the game, few beers in town then
back to the cock for the stag do/
hen party. Naomi insisted both
parties took place at the Cock so
she could keep an eye on Col and
also takings would be up.

The plan for the stag do was
simple. Meet in the Cock, have a
few liveners. Go to the Starfish
and Truffle for a few. Go watch
the match. Smash the Kidsgrove
fans, then back to the Cock for a
perfect stag night, i.e. Beer,
boobs, birds then a kebab on the
way home.

Naomi wanted it kept classy so
the strippers were only allowed
to do extras round the back of

the pub. She didn't want it to be some filthy night. I respected her for that.

The day arrived and the lads all met at the Cock for a few, The entire firm was out. Me, Mental, Shabba, Big Jock, Mongoose and Col. Proper tasty it was.

We went into town for the game and to have a few cheeky beers. On the way to the ground, we notice three lads from Kidsgrove. Perfect we thought so we ran at them and gave them a bit of a kicking, there was punches thrown, kicks going in. I manged to slap a lad across the face, before my asthma kicked in and I had to get my inhaler out and have a toot.

As I'm wheezing away, I notice a firm of lads charging towards us. Unfortunately, what with me not being able to breath I could warn the lads. And all hell broke loose. About fifty lads from Kidsgrove waded in and battered the living crap out of our lads. Shabba false teeth went flying. He hasn't seen them to this day. Mental took three lads down with him. I reckon they would have had a least a week off school to recover the injuries they received. Col battered a good few of their boys. Once my inhaler kicked in, I tried to assist the lads but it was a little difficult what with three girls and a skinny lad kicking seven bells out of me.

The kicking went on for minutes
then the police turned up and
they bolted, so result for BLT,
we stood our ground so win to us.
Mental got off the floor with a
semi on, he loved the old
violence. Col got a black eye and
mongoose ended up in A and E with
a head injury. To make matters
worse the game was shit, we lost.

Back at the Cock Naomi went
mental, her precious Col had a
split lip and a black eye. You
would have believed he had just
returned from the Falklands; the
fuss Naomi made. She slapped the
rest of us for not looking after
Col.

Not long later the disco started
and both the stags and Hens got
down to some serious partying.

The strippers that turned up we a
little rough, one of them was
Mongoose's mother. She's 67 and
looks like burns victim. But
Shabba rated her, said her extras
were amazing, he proudly told us
all she sucked him like a
Labrador eating a hot chip. So
can't slag her off.

The male strippers that arrived
were all muscle bound and oiled.
The girls were going crazy. Edda
who only weeks earlier had given
her virginity to me was acting
like a sexed crazed animal.
Unfortunately for the girls, the
person who placed the order for
the male strippers was Col. So,
the agency sent men that enjoyed
to company of other men, thinking
Col wanted the strippers for
himself. The girls had no chance

with them, Mental on the other hand was very popular.

The clues were there, they started stripping to 'Its Raining Men'

The girls weren't impressed and once Naomi had run the strippers out of the pub, she insisted that Me, Col and Mental make it up to her by putting on a show.

We didn't have baby oil, so we covered our bare chests in lager, and gave a half-hearted dance for the girls. Naomi jumped Col and dragged him into the toilets. We just carried on drinking and eating the finger buffet. The night went on for a while, Big Jock and Eileen had a barny about

something or other, it ended the
usual way, she slaps him a few
times, then starts crying telling
him she loved him.

Me and Edda got in about half
past four in the morning. Edda
was still a little turned on from
the performance I had given her,
and the fact I got the DJ to play
both the Lambada and Careless
Whisper so I could rub my semi up
and down her as we danced. Chicks
can't get enough of that lark.

Within minutes I was all over
Edda, I was fingering her like I
was grabbing change out of the
tray on the fruit machine. Before
you know it, I'm all sweaty and
wheezy and Edda is sexually
satisfied.

Away Day

Saturday morning arrived and the lads were all excited. Brompton away at Northwich. Big game for us. Turns out Northwich is sort just off the Broads so maybe have a few shandies down there and hire a boat, be a giggle. Anyway, we got a few cars and decided to go down, cause a bit of trouble then travel back.

In the Cockerel Mental is already at the bar, three pints in. Mongoose is well, pissed as a rat and Shaba was not far behind. So, I was driving to the game. I wasn't to bothered to be honest with you. I had promised Edda I would have a romantic night with

her when we got back, so I would
be better off not having a drink.

We set off for Northwich mid-
morning, as it turns out it isn't
near the Broads at all, we were
thinking of Norwich. Northwich is
actually near Chester. So, we
made a detour and decided to stop
at a service station for
refreshments and also Mental was
touching cloth.

So, I pulled in and parked up,
then went and had a mooch around.
Shabba was straight into the over
priced café, he could be heard
for miles shouting "How much."
When he was at the cash register,
trying to pay for a coffee and
sausage roll with a fiver.

After a few minutes I decided to
go back to the car, only problem
the car isn't there. I turned
around and its driving towards
the slip round. I turned and
bolted towards it. Luckily it
stopped. As I got to the car,
Shabba leans out of the driver's
side and just looks at me dead
calm like. "Oh, I thought you'd
gone." What a spanner, where the
hell did he think I had gone we
were on a bloody motorway.

So back in the car, I go, and off
we drive to Northwich. Once there
we got the news that the game had
been postponed due to half the
Brompton team having the shits.
They'd gone to Abbra Kebabra
after training the day before and
ordered a Magic Kebab, which is
Donar meat, chicken, lamb,

chicken tikka, chips, onion
rings, all covered in chilli
sauce, well they all got struck
down with a dodgy gut for some
reason.

We found a pub, a decent place,
type that has a real fire in it
and the barmaid had a full set of
dentures. We went in ordered a
few beers and sat around. The
landlord got chatting to us and
let us know there was a game of
football on at the local stadium.
Northwich ladies were playing
Swinton ladies.

We decided to go to the game and
support Swinton, have a laugh and
try and introduce a little
hooliganism to the lady's game.

Now it turns out we learnt a few
things about the lady's game.
One, no matter how many times you
chant get you tits out for the
lads', they don't. Two Chicks
football isn't too bad. Three
they don't swap shirts at the end
of the game, gutted.

They had a fair few supports at
Northwich so me and the lads
started giving it to them, trying
to get them going see if we could
have a tear up after the game. No
one seemed overly interested,
that is until Shabba starts
giving this lass some real abuse
about being a pig etc. You know
the sort of harmless banter one
has at the football. Unbeknown to
Shabba this lass is pre-menstrual
hence her dodgy mood.

She's losing the plot threatening Shabba, the works, her mates were holding her back, it was a right laugh. The game finishes and I think it was two nil, or four all I can't remember, it was a dull game, plus hooligans don't really go for the game. We walk out the ground and this bint is still giving it loads to Shabba. So, we start we some jovial chants and a few remarks about her lack of appearance. As we do, she is getting madder and madder. It was hilarious.

We left the ground got into the car and drove back to Brompton. Good day, saw some football and back in time to treat Edda to a few drinks, a bit of a disco, some nice curry and portion of chips at *Singh for your Supper.*

Then back to the flat for a ride and then sleep, perfect day.

There I am ready to go at 7.30, new Stone Islands top on, skinny jeans, and a nice drop of aftershave. I looked and felt great. Edda finally gets ready, she's wearing a tight fitting short dress, heels, and wearing some new perfume I blagged from Burglar Barry, 'Kylies Down Under'. She looked and smelt amazing.

Within minutes we are in the Cock and all hell has broken loose. Turns out the lass from the Northwich game had jumped in her car and followed us back home, she was in the Cock having a pint with Naomi.

She'd arrived in the bar, seen
Shabba, after head butting him
kicked seven shades out of him.
Paramedics said it was the worst
broken nose, cheek bone fracture
they'd ever seen. The lass,
apologised to Naomi for the fight
bought her a drink and
subsequently become the best of
friends.

Soon as I walked in, she clocked
me, and gave me a right smack
around the head, I went flying.
Then Naomi slapped me, for being
a 'sexist twat.' No sooner had I
come round then Edda is kicking
me in the balls for saying shit
to this lass.

Luckily after a few beers bought
by me I explain it was harmless
and I aint sexist, the chick

calms down become less
premenstrual and settles in the
Cock for the night.

Turns out though to be a cracking
night, we had some laughs, danced
along to the disco and then me
and Edda went for a curry. Top
night. The ride I got back home
helped ease the pain of being
bitch slapped by three woman and
having my balls stamped on,
repeatedly

Turns out the lass from Northwich
was a decent sort Naomi and her
are still in contact with each
other. And as it turns out she
wasn't pre-menstrual, she was
just moody because of the abuse
we gave her, what are the odds?

She has been back to the Cock
several times and is an alright
lass really. Decent sense of
humour and when she puts the
effort in, she's a bit of a
looker.

All Change

One morning after a vigerous
session in the Cock, and a fumble
with our lass, Edda walked into
the bedroom carrying two mugs of
tea. She stood there in just a
thong and t shirt, and smudged
make-up. Looking radiant and hot
as hell, the only thing was she
had developed a bit of a spunk
gut. You know, getting a bit
chubby. Being the decent fella, I
am I pointed it out to her. Well,
she didn't for some reason like
that and she properly sulked,
there were tears, snot and this
horrible wailing sounds. It
sounded like an old war time air
raid warning siren.

She kept that up for ages. Chicks can drag a mood on for ages. Eventually she calmed down and climbed into bed. She rolled over for a cuddle and I pretended I couldn't get my arms round her. Here we go again, the snot and tears, I am no woman doctor but I could tell she was in a mood. I was only happy I had scored with her the night before as it was obvious, she was getting pre-menstrual.

Eventually she calmed herself down and made us both a fresh cup of tea. With all her moaning and that mine had gone cold. We got chatting and eventually like the modern man I am I got round to asking her why she was a moody cow.

Without warning or any shame Edda
turned to me and announced that
she was in fact sticks up. That's
right pregnant, with a baby. I
went fucking mental. The nasty
mare had got herself knocked up
by some random cock. I was
fuming.

Turns out not as fuming as Edda
when she pointed out I was the
father, also the only man she had
ever been with and she most
definitely was not a cheating
slag. We both calmed down and
eventually saw the funny side of
it all, well I did.

Once the news had sunk in and
Edda had given me a hand job, you
know to celebrate the news, I got
up to go give the lads the good
news.

We arrived in the Glorious Cockerel just in time to witness Naomi throwing out Paedo Paul. Apparently, he had asked for a fresh glass and Naomi took it as a slur on her character.

Inside the bar, I waited for the place to go a little silent then announced that Edda was pregnant. You could hear a pin drop. Naomi, broke the silence by screaming "If I find out which one of you bastards has knocked this innocent girl up, I will knee cap you." then calmly and politely rubbed by back and gave me a free drink.

I smiled and said "no, I am the father." Naomi quickly snatched back my free pint and the place erupted with cheers and applause.

We stayed and had a good few
pints. During which time, one of
the lads from Worksop firm came
in. It turns out he was there to
fix the fruit machine, but me and
Mental clocked him. As soon as he
set to work on the machine, we
ran up behind him and started
giving him a right kicking. He
didn't stand a chance. We booted
the shit out of him, left him
there bleeding as we made our
exit, before police were called.

About half an hour later Edda
came back from the pub and told
me the lad from Worksop was
livid. He didn't like the fact we
jumped him, and he swore revenge.

That night in the bar having a
few cheeky drinks the lad rocks
up all by himself. I couldn't

believe the cheek of him. Me, Mongoose and Mental put our beers down and walked towards him. Soon as we got close enough, metal throws a massive punch at him. It was at this point that the door swung open and about thirty lads from Worksop came running in. Before you know it, I'm on the dance floor with five lads kicking me senseless. Mental is being torn limb from limb by about ten lads. Mongoose is hiding under the pool table with lads throwing pool balls at him. The only thing that stopped them was Naomi heard the fuss and came downstairs. The lads took one look at her and bolted.

I was black and blue. My balls took a right beating. Luckily, I had already knocked Edda up, so

not really an issue anymore.
Mental was buzzing, to him it was
a great start to the evening.
Naomi was a sweety she didn't
charge me for the ice to cool
down my balls, granted she
charged me two pounds for the
plastic bag to put the ice in.
But still a sweet thing to do.
The rest of the night was
ordinary. I was in too much pain
to enjoy a night on the ale.
However, I will point out doing
the lambada with aching balls is
no picnic.

Back at the flat Edda gave me a
rub down, shame she was pregnant
otherwise I would have given her
a length. You can't bang a
pregnant woman, not fair on the

unborn baby having my cock thrust
in its face, so we had to stick
to hand jobs and blowys for nine
months.

A few days later I'm down the
Cock having a swift lager top.
When Mental walks in. I was
dreading speaking with Mental I
had some news that was going to
destroy his world.

Mental wasn't in the best of
moods; I had never seen him so
low. Something was bothering him.
However, I promised Edda I would
speak with Mental so I went to
the bar and had a chat with him.

When I got to the bar Mental was
in pieces, really upset. Turns
out his benefits had been stopped

and he was deemed fit to work. Absolutely terrible news, I was gutted for him. He was a broken man, proper emotional.

Is there a worse sentence known to man, worse than 'you are fit to work.' Mental had got himself a job interview down at Buy the Way as their warehouse and distribution operative. Shelf stacker to you and me.

I gave him my bad news. That I promised Edda I would leave the firm and get a real job. Arthur down at 'We Are Rooting for You' garden centre had given me full time job and now the baby was on the way I had no choice.

I'm not scared to admit it, we both cried that morning.

We decided to leave on a high, Brompton were down to play Chesterfield in the next round of the cup so we would head and on our way stop off at Bramall Lane, and take on the BBC. Go out in a blaze of glory.

That was the plan and we set to work on it that very same day, after a few lagers obviously.

Retirement

The big day arrived. BLT versus
Sheffield United's BBC. Myself,
Mental, Mongoose and Shabba met
in the Glorious Cockerel. I was
wearing my favourite Stone
Islands sweatshirt. Mental was
head to toe in Fred Perry,
Mongoose looked like he had ram
raided Primemark and Shabba had
on his lucky raincoat.

We were all proper buzzing for
the day. We'd met the BBC before
on our away day to London, and to
be fair they ragged the shit out

of us. So on our way to Chesterfield it was revenge time. We knew some of their boys drank on London Road so we would head there, trash a pub or two then take on Chesterfield. Two for one if you like.

We left the Cock to a hero's goodbye the ladies were all there, excited for their men. We set off for our final day out as a firm and our biggest battle to date. It is how I imagined it looked when men marched off to go to war.

When we arrived on London Road, we realised two things one, it was a shit hole, two Sheffield United were away so smashing there pub up would be easier and more fun. We went into this pub

and it was dead, only a fat
barmaid and some shit music on
the jukebox. So, we ordered a
round of drinks and sat there.
Once we had finished, we went
into the gents' toilets and wrote
BLT all over the place it was
crazy, then Mental ripped the
hand dryer off the wall. We
walked out of the toilets and
threw the hand dryer behind the
bar and legged it all laughing as
we ran up the road.

Result Sheffield United seen off.
We headed to Chesterfield. That
place was a mess. Almost felt
sorry for the locals, knowing we
were going to smash their town
up.

We went to the game and let's be
fair it was crap. After the game

we went into the market square
found a pub and had a few beers.
We were just about to smash the
place up when it went a little
wrong for us. A load of Sheffield
United fans heard about their
local being smashed up, realised
we were in Chesterfield so they
came looking for us. Next thing
about twenty lads come steaming
into the pub. We of course denied
being from Brompton and sat there
whilst they looked angry and
marched off. Soon as the place
was clear, we legged it outside
smashed a few pint pots and
jumped into a taxi.

As we headed down the road, we
saw the United fans so we shouted
at them out of the windows and
gave them the wankers signs. It
was funny. It would have been

hilarious if it hadn't been for the red traffic lights. Soon as the taxi comes to a holt the United fans charge the taxi and we get a right kicking. Wankers took my trainers. That's twice after a ruck my trainers have been stolen.

After a quick visit to A&E we headed back home. Mental loved it; the taste of blood was like an aphrodisiac for him.

We headed home. Our last day as hooligans. Back in the Cock we were greeted as the hero's we were. Edda was dressed proper slutty for me. Shaniqua had on a number that left nothing to the imagination and the women of the bar were all in their finest most revealing outfits. That night was

a strange night, I was happy to
be in the Cock with my lass but I
knew that was it, my days of
being a hooligan came to an end.
It had been an exciting half a
season. I had some scrapes, saw
off some firms, and go myself a
regular bunk up. Edda looked
beautiful preggers, in tight
leggings. Her tits starting to
really take shape.

Do I regret life in the fast
lane? Hell, no it was a riot from
start to finish.

The future, well Mental went on
to study at college and qualified
as a doorman. He loves a fight
and working on the doors in town
helps him get his fix.

Mongoose left Brompton, he well, to be honest he got six years for his part in a drug deal that went massively wrong, but hey, they do when you try sell your gear to your cousin who also happens to be a police officer.

Naomi and Col are still at the Cockerel, still a lovely couple. We still go down every Friday and Saturday night, Edda goes to lady's night on a Wednesday and I get out for Pool night Tuesday oh and Sundays obviously. And now Edda has got her figure back we have regular bunk ups at the weekend. Edda now runs *For Eyes* the opticians in the high street and I luckily hurt my back first day at the garden Centre and now

can't work, and I get full
disability. Result. Edda and me
had a baby boy, we named him
after her dad Herman. His full
legal name Herman Daz Boot.

Looking back being a hooligan was
one of the best things I ever
did. I would highly recommend it.
But only to proper hard bastards
like myself.

As for the future, well I have it
sorted. Kid on our estate is a
whizz with computers and that. So
I am getting him to make me a
dating app for birds that like
hardmen, and hard men that like
birds that like hardmen. I'm
calling it Hoolifan™

See if you're in a firm, you put picture of yourself in your cool gear, you know a knock off Stone Island or Armani. Bang up another pic of you in the pub so she knows she is guaranteed a decent night out and maybe a picture of you in a fight or cut up after a fight so she knows you're a proper man. The girl sticks a pick up of her made up, and one with the boobs on show but not hanging out, you know looking pretty and that. So the man knows your up for a bunk up. I can see it now; I will be like that Jez Bazo fella from Amazon. I will make a mint. Obviously I wont deliver the bird in a van. I've been told that's trafficking and well dodgy, unless your rich or in the elite of society.

YOU'VE JUST HAD A
TASTE OF THE BLT

Brompton Life Takers

Robert E Harris:

Sir Winston 'Bulldog' Thatcher
KBE DSO QGM An Unauthorised
Autobiography.

Tales from the Terrace

Pop Kids.

Swipe Right?

Honourable.

D Coy.

Printed in Great Britain
by Amazon

16992658R00129